Island Dresses

by Roderick J. Robison

Contains excerpts from the story "Geni's Gulls" in *A Nature Trio: Three Stories for Children*. Reprinted with permission.

Also by Roderick J. Robison
The Lunch Lady's Daughter Series
The Magic Water
Middle School Millionaires
The Principal's Son
The Newbie
The Newbie 2

For my sister, Kristin, who once wore an "island dress"

And for my mother, who introduced us to island life

Chapter 1

Cheri McDaniel glanced up at the clock on the classroom wall. Less than a minute to go. Less than a minute until the final bell—and the beginning of summer vacation. Cheri had big plans for the summer. She and her best friend Kara had the summer all planned out. Everything was all set.

The two of them would be attending day camp. There would be field trips, arts & crafts, talent shows, swimming, sports and much more. On weekends they'd go to the town pool or the beach. Then there was the Fourth of July celebration and weekly movie night at the library. Yes sir. Summer was looking good. It was going to be the best summer yet.

Brriiiiinngg!

"Have a great summer, everyone," Mrs. Trisher said to her fifth grade students. "Good luck at middle school next fall."

Cheri got up and anxiously headed for the doorway with her classmates. She was the first one out the door. Summer vacation had officially begun!

*****

Her mother was in the kitchen when Cheri got home from school that day. Cheri knew from the look on her mother's face that something was up.

"Sit down," her mother said. "I have some *news*."

Cheri sat down at the kitchen table. "Good news?" she asked her mother.

Mrs. McDaniel nodded. "Yes. Very good news. I found a job—a fulltime position at the hospital. I'm starting work next Monday."

"That's great, Mom! Good for you." Cheri hugged her mother. She was truly happy for her mother. Her mother had been searching for a job for months.

"Thanks, sweetheart. There's more news too…You'll be staying with your Aunt Claire in Maine this summer."

Cheri frowned. "Mom, I have plans for the summer. Everything is all set. Kara and I are going to day camp. I need to stay here for the summer."

Her mother shook her head. "You're too young to stay at home on your own."

"But, Mom. I won't be on my own. I'll be at camp during the day," Cheri pleaded. "You won't need to be home if I'm at camp all day. Camp starts next week."

Her mother shook her head sideways. "I'm working nights for the summer, sweetheart. The night shift was the only one available. I'll be able to change over to the day shift in September."

"But, Mom!"

"You can go to camp next summer," her mother said. "I promise. Besides, I think you'll like what Aunt Claire has planned for you and your cousin Victor this summer. Did I mention that Victor is spending the summer with Aunt Claire too? Aunt Claire is really looking forward to spending some time with the two of you."

Cheri sighed. "What does Aunt Claire have *planned* for us?"

"She's bringing you and Victor to the island."

Oh no! "How long do we have to stay on the island for?"

Her mother smiled. "I think Aunt Claire plans to spend most of the summer on the island."

Ugh.

The family-owned island, Cheri knew, was located in Cobscook Bay off the coast of Maine. Cheri had been there once. The place was about as remote as it got. There was no electricity. No computers. No email. No television. No phone. No indoor plumbing.

She and her mother had spent a dismal weekend there a few summers before. It rained the entire time. They had been confined to the cabin throughout their stay.

"I don't want to go to the island!" Sarah pleaded.

Mrs. McDaniel looked at her daughter. "Sorry, sweetheart. This is not negotiable. Your bus ticket has been purchased. Your bus leaves at nine o'clock Saturday morning. Aunt Claire will pick

3

you up at the bus station in Bangor. Everything is all set. Things will turn out fine. You'll see."

Cheri couldn't believe it. Just minutes ago she had such high hopes for the summer. Now she was in for the most boring summer of her life!

Kara came over later that afternoon. Cheri broke the news to her best friend. "I'm not going to camp…I'm going to Maine for the summer…to live on an island."

"Cool," Kara replied. "You're lucky. My cousins go to Nantucket each summer. I've always been envious of them."

"This island *isn't* like Nantucket," Cheri said. "It's *tiny*. It's only seven acres. You can walk around it in less than an hour."

"Well, it still sounds cool to me."

"You don't understand," Cheri said. "The only people on the island will be my aunt, my cousin and I. There's one cabin on the whole island. That's it."

"So? I wouldn't mind that."

Cheri sighed. "The cabin doesn't even have indoor plumbing. There's no electricity. No internet. No computer. No phone."

"…Oh…That could be a problem."

Sleep did not come easy for Cheri that night. She tossed and turned. Leaving town for the summer was not a pleasant thought at all. Spending the summer on a remote island where there would be nothing to do was the last thing she wanted. And when the bus pulled into the station in Bangor, Maine, on Saturday afternoon, her mind hadn't changed.

Chapter 2

Cheri saw her aunt and cousin from the bus window as the driver pulled to a stop. Aunt Claire was wearing clothes from an earlier time—bellbottom jeans, an embroidered shirt and a leather fringed vest.

The two of them waved to Cheri. Both of them were smiling.

What is there to be happy about?

When Cheri stepped off the bus, Aunt Claire embraced her in a hug. "Good to see you, kiddo," she said.

"Hi, Aunt Claire."

Victor had a big grin on his face. Victor was a year younger than Cheri. "Hi, Cheri."

"Hey, Vic."

The bus driver disembarked from the bus and opened the luggage compartment on the side of the bus. "Let's get your luggage," Aunt Claire said. "We've got some traveling ahead of us today."

"Where are we headed?" Cheri inquired.

"To the island."

"We're going to the island *today*?" Cheri asked. She had already spent more than four hours on the road. What was the hurry?

"That's right," Aunt Claire confirmed. "We should be able make it to the island just before sundown if we leave now."

Great. I can't wait.

They grabbed Cheri's duffel bag and backpack from the luggage compartment and headed over to the parking lot. Aunt Claire's aging van was easy to spot—it was the one with a boat trailer hitched up behind it. Secured to the trailer was a fourteen-foot aluminum boat with an old Johnson outboard motor.

When they reached the van, Aunt Claire opened the side door. The van was jam packed. It was filled with stuff—sleeping bags, pillows, water jugs, coolers, groceries, fishing rods, pots & pans, duffel bags, oars, rope, life jackets, a camp stove, folding chairs, tarps, hip boots, tools, and a tent.

"What's with the tent?" Cheri asked.

Aunt Claire smiled. "It's a backup."

"A backup?"

Aunt Claire nodded. "In case the cabin is not…habitable. Depending on what the winter was like, the cabin may need some *work* before we can move in."

Ugh. Cheri was *not* a camper.

They crammed Cheri's backpack and duffel bag into the back of the van. Then everyone hopped in and Aunt Claire pulled away from the bus station. Soon they were headed north on Route 1 where they caught glimpses of the Atlantic Ocean along stretches between small coastal towns. As they made their way up the coast, they passed by picturesque farmlands, old homesteads, antique shops and tourist attractions, but Cheri didn't take in any of the scenery.

She inserted her earbuds in her ears, listened to her favorite song, and texted Kara. Cheri was brooding. She was constantly thinking about all the fun she'd be missing out this summer. Meanwhile, Victor read a book on fossils and Aunt Claire hummed the lyrics to songs from an earlier decade as they slowly weaved their way up the coast.

After what seemed like forever, Aunt Claire turned off Route 1 and headed down State Route 190. Ten minutes later, the van turned off the road and they entered a small coastal town. The town was nothing like the town Cheri lived in. This town had a population of just 698 people according to a sign at the top of Main Street.

There were just a dozen businesses in the "downtown" area. All of them were located on Main Street. There was a grocery store, a laundromat, a hardware store, a diner, a gas station, two restaurants, a movie theater, a book store, a dime store, a thrift shop and a real estate office. Two streets above Main Street were a library, a community center, and an elementary school.

They passed through the town before they knew it. Aunt Claire continued down Main Street and five minutes later she pulled onto an unmarked gravel road. The road wound through a thick stand of pine trees before ending at a grassy campground along the edge of Cobscook Bay. There was mist in the air and fog was rolling in from the bay.

"Time to fill the water jugs," Aunt Claire announced as she pulled the van up to a small outbuilding.

Aunt Claire and Victor hopped out of the van. They removed four plastic water jugs from the back of the van and brought them over to the spigot on the side of the building. While Victor and Aunt Claire filled the water jugs, Cheri remained in the van. She wanted to text Kara. But the screen on her cell phone read NO SERVICE. Cheri sighed. How could she get by without texting and talking on her cell phone for a whole summer? Using her cell phone was something she had always taken for granted. She didn't know how she was going to get by without it.

I want to go home!

Victor and Aunt Claire loaded the water jugs into the boat. Then they got back in the van and Aunt Claire drove over to a small boat launch ramp on the opposite side of the campground. She backed the van up to the water's edge and engaged the emergency brake.

Aunt Claire and Victor got out and donned hip boots. Cheri watched as they made quick work of loosening the trailer's winch. The boat slid off the trailer into the water. Once the boat was in the water, Aunt Claire and Victor began to unload everything from the van.

"Cheri," Aunt Claire called. "We could use your help."

Cheri frowned. She stepped out of the van and traded her sneakers for an old pair of hip boots as her aunt pulled the van away from the boat launch ramp and parked it up on high ground. Cheri helped her cousin load the boat. When Aunt Claire returned five minutes later she was pleased to see that everything had been loaded into the boat. She handed out life jackets. Once everyone had a life jacket on she said, "All aboard, the water taxi is departing."

Victor eagerly hopped into the boat and claimed the middle seat. Cheri reluctantly boarded the craft and took a seat on a pile of coiled rope up front in the bow. Aunt Claire pushed the boat off from shore and hopped in the stern. Then she pulled the outboard motor's starter cord. The motor sputtered for a few seconds and conked out.

"Victor, man the oars."

Cheri winced. She had visions of rowing all the way out to the island—it would take hours to reach the island if they had to row there. Aunt Claire pulled the starter cord again. The engine sputtered…and conked out again.

This is not looking good.

Aunt Claire pulled the starter cord once more…The engine started. "Yahoo!"

Victor placed the oars in the boat and they were off. They headed across Cobscook Bay…into the fog.

Fifteen minutes later the fog was so thick they couldn't see more than thirty yards ahead…There was no sign of the island. Aunt Claire cut the power to the outboard motor. The boat drifted in the fog.

Great! Now we're lost at sea.

Aunt Claire stared into the mist. She cupped her hand behind her right ear and listened.

"What are you doing?" Cheri asked.

"She's listening," Victor explained.

"What do you expect to hear?"

"Seagulls," Aunt Claire answered.

"Huh?"

"Listen."

The faint sound of seagulls could be heard to the west. "Time to row, Victor. Row toward the seagulls. Row toward the seagulls and we'll find the island. Seagulls nest on the island."

Victor rowed. Soon the cries of seagulls became louder. Then the island's eastern shoreline loomed into view. Cheri breathed a sigh of relief as she took in the view.

A rocky beach stretched along the island's eastern coastline. Along the top edge of the beach was a band of dark seaweed that had washed ashore. Above that was a thick strip of green sea peas and beyond that a hill. The hill was located in the island's central region, the island's highest terrain. The top of the hill was obscured by fog, but the flat land of the island's northern region was visible.

The island's northernmost section was as Cheri remembered it: rocky terrain interspersed with small patches of vegetation—weeds, raspberry bushes, thistle, and gooseberry bushes. There were several stands of stunted pine trees too.

Cheri couldn't make out the southern end of the island through the mist. She hadn't ventured to the southern part of the island on her previous trip. She recalled the area was covered by dense growth. The place had seemed uninhabitable.

Five minutes later, Victor pulled the boat up to the small dock on the island's eastern shoreline. Then he and Aunt Claire hopped out onto the dock. Victor tied the boat lines to a piling while Aunt Claire pulled the motor up. Cheri felt left out. She sat in the boat by herself while her cousin and aunt went about their tasks. This was all so new to her; she knew nothing about boats.

"Let's bring a load up to the cabin and see how it fared over the winter," Aunt Claire said.

"When were you last on the island?" Cheri asked.

"About a year ago."

Oh no.

On the way up the hill the sun began to break through the fog. Then the fog started to dissipate and they could make out the cabin on the high ground at the center of the island. When they reached the cabin nobody said a word. The three of them just stared at it. Shingles had blown off during the winter and lay scattered on the ground around the perimeter of the cabin. And the front door was open.

"Looks like last winter was a tough one," Aunt Claire remarked. She removed a flashlight from her pack. "Let's go inside and check it out."

Aunt Claire headed into the cabin through the front doorway. Cheri and Victor tentatively followed her inside. The window shields were still in place and the cabin was dark inside. As their eyes adjusted to the dim light they saw the floor was covered with debris the wind had blown in over the winter— seaweed, brush and weeds.

Suddenly there was a rustling noise at the back of the cabin. Cheri had never been so scared. She bolted out of the cabin. Victor and Aunt Claire were right behind her…A seagull flew out the doorway behind them.

"Well," Aunt Claire remarked after they caught their breath outside. "Just an old seagull. I hope that was the only one inside the cabin."

Cheri could still feel her heart thudding.

"It's a bit too late to clean the cabin up today," Aunt Claire declared. "Let's pitch the tent and set up camp."

Great.

The three of them hauled the water, provisions, sleeping bags and other gear, and their belongings up from the boat. Then

Victor and Cheri set up the tent while Aunt Claire got a campfire going to cook dinner. Night had fallen by the time dinner was ready.

The three of them sat on stump stools around the campfire as they ate their dinner—baked beans, hot dogs, and canned brown bread.

It started to rain as Cheri took her last bite.

Wonderful.

Chapter 3

Cheri was the only one in the tent when she woke the following morning. The aroma of bacon and eggs wafted in through the tent's mesh screen door. Cheri got up and stretched. Then she stepped outside. The sky had cleared during the night. She squinted at the sunlight; it was a beautiful day with just a slight wind.

The view from the campsite was remarkable. The entire bay stretched out before her. There was hardly any wind and the water was glasslike. Several harbor seals basked in the sun on rock ledges just offshore. Flocks of eider ducks traded up and down the bay, flying low to the water. And seagulls were everywhere—in the air, in the water, on top of rocks, and perched on low lying branches of stunted pine trees. The air was filled their cries.

Cheri looked up the bay and took in the other islands. There were a few fishing boats and sail boats beyond the islands. The visibility was so good that she could make out some of the cottages along the shoreline of the mainland.

Aunt Claire was kneeling by the campfire preparing breakfast in a cast iron skillet. "Good morning, there."

"Morning," Cheri said.

Aunt Claire stood up and looked northward. "It's so clear today you can see Campobello," she said.

"Campobello?"

"Campobello Island," Aunt Claire remarked. "It's in Canada."

"Wow," Cheri said. "I didn't realize we were so far north."

Aunt Claire nodded and pointed up the bay. "That's Campobello," she said.

Cheri looked where her aunt was pointing. "Aah. I see it."

"President Roosevelt used to spend summers there," Aunt Claire informed her. "There's a park named after him on the island. And a bridge too."

"Huh…Where's Victor?"

"He's down at the shoreline gathering firewood. Gathering firewood is a daily chore out here."

Aunt Claire placed two pieces of bacon, toast and scrambled eggs on a plate. Then she handed the plate to Cheri. "Here you go."

"Thanks, Aunt Claire."

"You're welcome. Eat up. We've got work to do."

"Work?"

Aunt Claire nodded. "We need to clean the cabin. And there are shingles to replace. But first things first. After breakfast we need to go down to the beach to get buckets of seawater."

"Seawater? What do we need seawater for?"

"We use seawater for cleaning. Fresh water is too precious to waste."

So much for a relaxing vacation.

Victor returned with a load of firewood a few minutes later. He set the firewood down and took a seat on a stump stool by the campfire. "I'm starved."

Aunt Claire handed him a plate of breakfast. "Here you go."

"Thanks, Aunt Claire!"

"My pleasure."

The three of them went to work after breakfast. First they removed the window shields from the cabin and picked up the cedar shingles that had blown off during the winter. Then Aunt Claire donned a nail apron, grabbed a hammer from her tool box, and nailed the shingles back into place with Victor's help. After that they swept the cabin out and splashed buckets of seawater on the wooden kitchen table, handcrafted chairs, fishnet cots, and shelves. Then they washed windows and scrubbed the cabin's walls and plank floor.

By three o'clock the one-room cabin was habitable. They brought their gear in, rolled out their sleeping bags on the fishnet cots and finally settled in.

*****

Aunt Claire served dinner at the cabin's only table that evening. The table faced the cabin's side window. All three of them stared out at the view as they ate. The day's final rays of sunlight flickered on the bay. A pair of harbor seals swam along the island's shoreline. A Great Blue Heron stalked the shallows in the tidal pool in search of dinner. And what happened next took Cheri by surprise…Seagulls began landing in the clearing beside the cabin. One after the other. Beautiful birds with snow-white breast feathers and vibrant yellow beaks. Soon there were two dozen gulls in the clearing. Mother gulls.

They cocked their heads and cried out to call in their young for their daily meal. Young gray-colored gulls left their hiding places and came scurrying down trails in the fireweed that bordered the clearing. When they reached the clearing the young gulls eagerly made their way over to their mothers for their daily meal—shrimp.

As much as she didn't want to be there, Cheri had to admit the scene was kind of cool. It was as if they had their own nature channel.

"How do the young gulls know which gull is their mother?" Cheri asked. "All of the adult gulls look the same."

"Each mother gull calls to her young from the same spot each evening," Victor informed her. "The young gulls know the spot well."

"How do you know this?"

Victor smiled. "I asked Aunt Claire the same question when I was here last summer. You'll see. Tomorrow night each of the mother gulls will feed their young in the same place."

"That's right," Aunt Claire confirmed. "The young gulls meet their mother at the same spot each evening for their supper. I suspect that each mother gull has her own distinctive feeding call too."

The sun began to edge down over the horizon as the young gulls in the clearing devoured their meal. After all of the young gulls finished their meal, they gradually retreated back to their hiding places in the fireweed to settle down for the night.

After dinner Aunt Claire boiled a pot of seawater on the tabletop camp stove for cleaning the dishes. Then she lit the kerosene lamps. After that she turned on the transistor radio…but there was no sound. The batteries were dead. "Well, we'll have to add batteries to the shopping list when we go to town," she stated.

Cheri rolled her eyes. No electricity. No indoor plumbing. No phone. The radio was their only link to the world but it didn't even work. "When are we going to town?" she asked.

"The day after tomorrow. We have enough food and water to get by until then."

Cheri looked around the room. It was too early to go to bed. How she longed for a television. And running water. And a phone. She was so accustomed to calling Kara after dinner. "There's nothing to do," she complained.

Aunt Claire looked over at her. "Read."

"Huh?"

"There are plenty of books to read," her aunt said. She motioned to the bookshelf across the room beside the Franklin wood stove. "Your mother and I read Nancy Drew mysteries when we were your age. There's a whole bunch of them on the shelf. And there are other books too—like the Outdoor Girl series and Beverly Gray mysteries. You won't be at a loss for reading material out here."

Cheri sighed. She couldn't remember the last time she read a book for pleasure. She walked over to the bookshelf and perused the titles. A few minutes later she removed a Nancy Drew mystery and brought it over to the table.

She pulled up a chair. Then she sat down and opened the book...Before Cheri knew it she was on page twenty-five. She was curious as to how Nancy Drew would be able to find a hidden message in a hollow oak tree. Aunt Claire interrupted her thoughts with an announcement. "It's been a long day. I'm turning in."

"Me too," Victor yawned.

Cheri closed her book. Then the three of them went outside to brush their teeth. When they returned to the cabin, Aunt Claire said, "Okay, lights out. See you two in the morning."

As she drifted off to sleep that night, Cheri found herself still wondering how Nancy Drew would find a hidden message in a hollow oak tree.

Chapter 4

Once again, Cheri was the last one to wake up the following morning. She squinted at the sunlight streaming in through the cabin's side window as she climbed out of her sleeping bag.

She got up and made her way over to the front door and opened it. Aunt Claire was cooking breakfast over a campfire. She smiled when she saw Cheri standing in the cabin's doorway. "Good morning."

"Morning," Cheri responded. "Where's Victor?"

"He's beachcombing."

"*Beachcombing?*" Cheri had never heard the term.

"He's walking around the shoreline to see what washed up overnight."

"Stuff washes up on the island?"

Aunt Claire smiled. "Yes. All kinds of things wash up here. You wouldn't believe some of the things that have washed up on the island over the years. We've found all sorts of things: lobster floats, lobster traps, fishing lures, logs, wooden fish boxes, furniture, bottles with notes in them, sections of docks and boats, boat cushions, oars, rope, lumber—you name it. Your mother and I even found an outhouse washed up once."

"Huh."

"Breakfast won't be ready for a while," Aunt Claire said. "You could probably catch up with Victor down at the beach. I don't think he's made it all the way around the island yet."

Cheri shrugged. "Okay."

"Have fun. And keep an eye out for firewood."

"Will do."

*****

Cheri caught up with Victor at the island's northern tip. He was dragging a large tree branch that had washed up on shore overnight. He was smiling; he was always smiling it seemed. The kid was in his element.

"What are you going to do with that?" Cheri inquired.

"I'm going to cut it up for firewood."

"Oh."

"I'm hungry," Victor said. "Let's go up to the cabin for breakfast."

The two of them headed back toward the cabin. They walked along the island's rocky shoreline for a while and then made their way up to the high ground. There was a seagull nesting area on the high ground in a small clearing. It was not too far from the cabin. There were a dozen nests on the ground in the nesting area. Each nest contained three eggs.

As the cousins neared the nesting area, a flock of crows flew overhead...The next thing they knew the crows were landing in the nesting area. Victor suddenly stopped and dropped the branch he had been dragging. He yelled, "No!"

Victor bolted for the nesting area. Cheri ran after him, though she had no idea why they were running. They reached the nesting area seconds later...The crows were making their way toward the nests. One crow was just two feet away from a nest.

"Leave them alone!" Victor yelled.

The crows cawed. Then they lifted off the ground and flew away. "They were after the eggs," Victor informed Cheri. "Crows are fond of seagull eggs."

"Oh."

"We need to protect the eggs," Victor stated. "Those crows flew over from the mainland. I'm sure they'll be back."

"We can't exactly stay here and watch the nests all day," Cheri said.

"No...but we could make a scarecrow. A scarecrow would probably keep the crows away."

"Hmmm...Good idea."

When they got back to the cabin, Aunt Claire had breakfast ready—pancakes. Victor and Cheri told her about the crows. "We're going to make a scarecrow to keep the crows away," Victor informed his aunt.

"That's a great idea," Aunt Claire replied. "There are some *island clothes* in the trunk underneath my cot. You can use some of them for the scarecrow."

"*Island clothes*?" Cheri asked. "What are *island clothes*?"

Aunt Claire smiled. "Old clothes. Clothes that have seen better days."

"Oh."

"You'll find some dresses in the trunk. Your mother and I wore them when we were your age. The dresses are all yours. Help yourself."

Cheri winced. "Uh, no thanks." She hadn't worn a dress since kindergarten. What was her aunt thinking? Dresses may have been fashionable when her mother and aunt were her age—but that had been a different lifetime!

"I'll get you some thread and a needle," Aunt Claire offered. "You'll want to sew the scarecrow's shirt to its pants."

"Thanks."

After breakfast, Cheri made her way over to her aunt's cot and pulled the trunk out from underneath it. She lifted the trunk's lid and peered inside. There were old jeans, a few pillow cases, faded sweat shirts, an old felt hat, flannel shirts…and five cotton dresses. Some were plain; others had faded floral patterns. *Ugh.*

Cheri pulled out a pair of old jeans and a faded flannel shirt. Then she shut the trunk and she and Victor got started on the scarecrow. They stuffed the old pair of jeans and flannel shirt with dried out seaweed they found down on the beach. Then Cheri fastened the pants to the shirt with the thread and a needle provided by Aunt Claire while Victor scrounged through the wood pile for stakes to prop the scarecrow up with.

"The scarecrow needs a head," Victor said when he returned from the wood pile. "Otherwise, the crows will know it's an imposter. Crows have good vision."

Aunt Claire had set up her easel in front of the cabin. She was within earshot and overheard the conversation as she mixed paint on a palette. "There are some old pillow cases in the trunk," she said. "You can stuff one. We'll paint a face on it."

"Thanks, Aunt Claire. Good idea."

Aunt Claire nodded. "You'll need a hat too. Your grandfather's old felt fedora hat is in the trunk. Grab it and we'll pin it to the scarecrow's head."

"Be right back," Victor said. "I'll get some more seaweed to stuff the scarecrow's head with."

"I'll get the pillow case and hat," Cheri offered.

"Sounds like a plan," Aunt Claire said.

Chapter 5

"This should work well," Victor said as he and Cheri tied the scarecrow to a stake that Victor had pounded into the ground at the edge of the nesting area. "I hope the scarecrow will fool the crows."

The two of them stepped back and looked the scarecrow over. Aunt Claire had painted a face on the pillow case. The scarecrow had blue eyes, dark eyebrows, a medium-size nose, big ears, and a wide grin. As a final touch, Cheri had pinned her grandfather's old felt fedora hat on the scarecrow's head. "I think it will do," she said.

"I hope so."

"What are you going to do now?" Cheri asked Victor.

"It's low tide. I'm going clamming."

"Clamming?" Cheri had never heard the word.

Victor flashed a smile. "I'm going to dig clams for dinner. Come with me."

"Okay."

They went up to the cabin and pulled on hip boots. Then Cheri followed Victor out back to the tool bin. Victor grabbed two clam rakes and a bucket. Then he said, "Let's go get dinner."

"Have fun," Aunt Claire shouted as they headed off to the clam flats.

"We will!"

They headed downhill to the shoreline in front of the cabin, crossed the rocky beach and headed out onto the flats. The tide was dead low—perfect for clamming. The flats were expansive—there was nearly a quarter mile of flats between the rocky beach and the water's edge.

Cheri followed her cousin across the flats. Victor seemed to have a particular location in mind. He headed toward a tidal pool on the westernmost section of the flats. When they neared the tidal pool, Victor dropped the clam rakes and bucket. "I had good luck at this spot last summer," he said.

Victor studied the mud as if he were looking for something in particular. Then he kneeled down and picked up a clam rake. Cheri watched as her cousin pushed the clam rake into the mud and raked through it. A few minutes later he said, "Found one!"

Victor reached down into the mud and pulled out a clam. He held it up and showed it to Cheri before he tossed it into the bucket.

Cheri kneeled down a few yards from Victor and picked up a clam rake. She pushed the rake into the mud.

"Found another one," Victor announced. He pulled a second clam from the mud and dropped it into the bucket.

Cheri raked through the mud looking for clams. She kept at it for ten minutes. Her arms were cached in mud. There was mud smeared on her face and neck too. But she had nothing to show for it. She hadn't found a single clam. During that time, Victor had pulled five more clams from the mud. He looked over at Cheri. "No luck?"

Cheri sighed. "No. What's your secret?"

"I don't have a secret," Victor said. "I just dig when I see an air hole."

"What's an air hole?"

Victor got up and made his way over to Cheri. He pointed to a small hole in the mud. "That is an air hole," he said. "There is a clam below it for sure."

Cheri placed her rake over the hole and plunged it into the mud. She excavated the mud slowly, removing a little more muck each time she raked. Soon, she spotted the white tip of a shell sticking up through the mud. "Found one!"

"All right!" Victor said.

Victor moved back to his spot and Cheri continued to ply the mud with her clam rake. She soon found a second clam. And then another…

Cheri grew bored after placing her tenth clam in the bucket. She got up, walked down to the tidal pool and waded in. The water was only a foot deep. It was crystal clear. The bottom of the tidal pool was covered with rocks. Many of the rocks were covered with limpets and sea urchins. Cheri stepped around them as she waded through the tidal pool. Small schools of minnows darted before her as she made her way across the tidal pool.

When she neared the center of the pool, an orange object in the water caught her attention. Cheri made her way over to it. She had never seen a starfish up close before. She was admiring the starfish when a flock of seagulls out in the bay caught her attention.

The gulls were squawking up a storm. They were hovering over the bay just offshore. Cheri noticed that the patch of water directly below gulls was darker than the surrounding water. It was churned up as if something just below the surface had suddenly come to life. Then she saw a school of shrimp jump out of the water and the water churned even more.

"Victor! What's that?" Cheri asked, pointing to the dark rough water below the gulls.

Victor looked over. "Holy mackerel! I'll be right back! Keep your eye on the gulls!"

"What's out there?"

"Mackerel!"

Cheri kept her eyes on the gulls as they moved back and forth over the school of mackerel. When the school of mackerel moved, the gulls did too. Sometimes the gulls would drop straight down into the water and then dart back up.

The next thing Cheri knew, Victor was running toward her in his hip boots. He was holding two spinning rods. When he reached her, he handed her a rod and said, "Follow me."

Though nearly out of breath, Victor bolted around the tidal pool and made his way to the water's edge. The flock of seagulls was even closer to shore now. They were more stirred up than ever, squawking and dive bombing into the school of mackerel. The water churned in a feeding frenzy.

Both rods were rigged with mackerel jigs—shiny diamond-shaped lures. Victor flipped the bail on his spinning reel and cast the mackerel jig…It landed in the center of the patch of rough water. As soon as he started to reel in, his rod bent. "Fish on!"

Cheri watched in awe as Victor struggled to reel in line. It seemed every time he reeled in a length of line, the mackerel would make a run and strip even more line from the reel. It was like a tug-of-war between the two of them. Victor battled the fish for five minutes before pulling it onto shore. The mackerel was magnificent. It was torpedo-shaped and very colorful—a combination of blue, black and silver. Its scales glistened in the sun.

The school of mackerel had moved farther from shore while Victor played the fish. The mackerel were beyond casting distance now. "How come you didn't try to catch one?" Victor asked.

Cheri shrugged. "Don't know how. I've never been fishing before."

Victor nodded. "I'll teach you how to cast later. The tide's coming in now. Let's bring the fish and clams up to the cabin."

*****

Aunt Claire was painting at her easel in front of the cabin when they got back. Her eyes opened wide when she saw the mackerel and the bucket of clams. "Well, it looks like it will be seafood for dinner tonight thanks to you two. Now we just need something for dessert."

"There are some raspberries down at the point," Victor said.

Aunt Claire smiled. "If you two would like to pick some, we can make raspberry cobbler for dessert."

"We're on it," Victor said. "Right Cheri?"

Cheri nodded. "Yes. I like raspberries."

Chapter 6

The raspberry bushes were full of berries...but not many of the berries were ripe. It was still early in the season. They were barely able to pick a pint between them. "This should hopefully be enough," Cheri said.

"Yep," Victor agreed. "Let's bring the berries to Aunt Claire."

They walked by the nesting grounds to check on the scarecrow on the way back to the cabin ...A seagull was perched on top of the fedora hat on the scarecrow's head.

"That's not good," Victor commented. "If the crows see that gull perched on the scarecrow they'll know it's a fake right away."

"You're right. But how can we keep the gulls from standing on the scarecrow's head?"

"I don't know," Victor said. "But we have to come up with something soon. The crows are gone for now, but they will be back for sure. They head over from the mainland every morning."

"Maybe Aunt Claire will know what to do."

"Yes, let's go see her."

*****

"Well, that's not good," Aunt Claire remarked when they broke news about the gull perched on top of the scarecrow.

"Any ideas?" Cheri asked.

Aunt Claire looked around. She seemed lost in thought for a few moments. Then her eyes focused on the scrap pile behind the cabin. In the pile were items that had washed up on shore over the years: old boards, a few broken chairs, an old broom, damaged fish baskets, broken lobster traps, old rope, stumps, scraps of fishnet…and a sheet of tin.

"I have an idea," Aunt Claire announced. "We'll make a *new* hat for the scarecrow."

"That won't work," Victor said. "Seagulls will stand on it just like now."

"They won't be able to stand on the hat I have in mind."

"Huh?"

"We'll make a tin hat for the scarecrow," Aunt Claire explained. "A pointed tin hat—like a witch's hat. Gulls can't perch on a pointed hat."

"Oh. Good idea."

Aunt Claire removed a pair of tin snips and a roll of heavy duty tape from the tool box. Then the three of them headed over to the scrap pile. Aunt Claire worked the tin snips and cut a triangle-shaped section from the sheet of tin. Then she rolled it into a cone and taped the seam to keep it from unraveling. The cone-shaped hat did indeed resemble a witch's hat, with the exception of its color. The top of the hat came to a perfect point.

"That should do it," Aunt Claire said. She handed the hat to Cheri. "Seagulls won't be able to perch on your scarecrow now. Your scarecrow is no longer an ordinary scarecrow."

"That's right," Victor said. "We now have a *witch* scarecrow." Victor picked up an old broom from the scrap pile. "And every witch needs a broom."

"That's right," Aunt Claire declared. "But don't take too long putting the hat on your scarecrow. It's getting late. Dinner will be ready soon."

"Be right back."

*****

It wasn't hard to secure the tin hat to the scarecrow's head. Cheri and Victor made quick work of it. Once the hat was secure they headed back to the cabin for dinner.

When they got back to the cabin, Aunt Claire had dinner on the table: steamed clams over linguine, a plate of smoked mackerel, and a bowl of garden salad. She handed each of them a plate. "Help yourselves. You two must be famished after your busy day."

Victor nodded. "I'm starved."

"Me too," Cheri admitted.

Like the previous evening, the view through the cabin's side window was spectacular. The day's final rays of sunlight flickered on the bay as a pair of harbor seals swam along the island's western shoreline and the mother gulls began landing in the clearing beside the cabin. They cocked their heads and called in their young for their daily meal. Young, gray-colored gulls scurried down trails in the fireweed and made their way to the clearing for their dinner.

What Victor had said at dinner the night before about the mother gulls feeding their young in the same place each evening was true, Cheri noted. She recalled a mother gull feeding her three young gulls by a jagged rock at the edge of the clearing the previous evening. And there they were now—a mother gull and her three young ones. Right by the jagged rock.

As Cheri, Victor and Aunt Claire finished their meal, the sun began to disappear over the horizon, and the young gulls returned to their hiding places in the fireweed to bed down for the night. Aunt Claire lit the kerosene lanterns and served raspberry cobbler for dessert.

After dessert, Cheri removed her Nancy Drew mystery from the book shelf and brought it over to the table. She picked up where she left off the night before. Victor set up his marbles on the floor in front of the wood stove. Aunt Claire started reading a novel.

Cheri's eyelids grew heavy after a few pages. It had been a busy day. Gathering firewood, beachcombing, chasing crows, constructing a scarecrow, clamming, exploring the tidal pool, fishing and berry picking had taken a toll. Cheri never had time to think about what she was missing out on back home. She yawned. "I'm turning in."

"Me too," Victor stated. He yawned too.

Aunt Claire looked up from her novel. "That's a good idea. We have a busy day ahead of us tomorrow. Sleep well."

Chapter 7

Aunt Claire was up earlier than usual the following morning. But Cheri and Victor did not wake to the aroma of bacon and eggs or pancakes. On the table were three bowls of cereal and three glasses of orange juice—powdered orange juice.

"We need to get an early start in order to make it back at high tide," Aunt Claire informed them.

In the weeks ahead, Cheri and Victor would learn that their aunt always planned trips to town around the tide. The return trip to the island worked best at high tide. When the tide was high you didn't have to haul groceries and water jugs as far. And you didn't have to worry about spilling the groceries on the mud flats which were exposed at low tide.

After a quick breakfast, they hauled the empty water jugs down to the boat. There was no fog, and they could just make out the campground from the island's eastern shore as they shoved off. Aunt Claire pulled the motor to life once they were in deep water.

The sky was overcast. It was windier than the past few days, but the winds were coming from the west and would be at their backs on the trip over to the mainland.

It took them just twenty minutes to reach the campground. Everybody hopped out of the boat. Victor carried the anchor up the rock beach and placed it above the high tide mark. Then the three of them carried the water jugs over to the spigot and filled them. After that they loaded the water jugs into the van and drove to town.

When they reached the town, Aunt Claire pulled the van into the parking lot in front of the grocery store. "I'll pick up the groceries," she said. "You two can check out the town if you like. Maybe visit some stores or go to the library. Let's meet back here in an hour. We'll get lunch down at the hotdog stand on the pier."

"Okay," Cheri said. "I'm going to the library. I need to use their computer. I want to e-mail my friend."

"I'll go with you," Victor said.

"All right. See you two in an hour."

The library was housed in an old two-story brick building. It looked more like a house than a library, Cheri thought. The library back home was about ten times as big.

There was an elderly woman at the front desk when they stepped inside. "Good morning, there!" she boomed.

"Hi," Cheri said.

"Hello," Victor put in.

"Where are you two from?" the woman asked. "I don't believe I've seen you folks before."

"I'm from Massachusetts," Cheri said.

"Rhode Island," Victor stated.

"Well, it's good to have you here."

"Thanks," Cheri replied. "Could I use the computer?"

The woman shook her head. "We don't have one."

"You *don't* have a computer?"

"No. We do things the old way."

Cheri sighed.

"What did you want to use a computer for?" the woman asked.

"I want to e-mail my friend."

The woman smiled. "I've got plenty of stationary if you'd like to write your friend a letter. The post office is just up the street."

"No, thanks," Cheri said.

"We have a nice selection of books," the woman offered.

"Uh, no thanks. We have plenty of books already."

"Very well."

"Thanks anyhow," Victor said. "See you later."

"Bye now. Thanks for stopping by."

The sky was darker when they stepped outside. And the wind had picked up. Several merchants were boarding up store windows along Main Street. Other merchants were pulling display items off the sidewalk. Pedestrians seemed to be walking faster than normal. It seemed as if everyone was in a hurry to get somewhere. Strange.

The cousins stopped in the dime store and bought penny candy. Then they headed over to the grocery store.

When they stepped inside the grocery store, the place was bustling with activity. There were lines of people with overloaded shopping carts at each cash register. A lot of shopping carts contained bottled water and batteries. Aunt Claire was waiting in line at the middle cash register. "Hey, you two," she called out when she saw them. "Did you e-mail your friend, Cheri?"

Cheri shook her head. "The library doesn't have a computer. Can you believe it?"

Aunt Claire nodded. "That's not surprising. You could write your friend a letter you know."

"That's what the librarian said."

The person in front of them paid the cashier and pushed their cart forward. "How about helping your aunt unload these groceries?"

"Sure," Victor said. He took charge of unloading the items in the cart and placed them on the conveyor belt as Aunt Claire made her way over to the cashier.

"You folks ready for the storm?" the cashier asked.

Aunt Claire's eyebrows lifted. "*Storm*?"

"You haven't heard about the storm?" the cashier inquired.

Aunt Claire shook her head. "No. We've been a bit out of touch the past few days. The batteries in our radio died."

"Well, it's going to be a big one. They say it could be the worst storm to hit these parts in decades. Wasn't a big deal a few days ago but the storm has suddenly intensified. Gale force winds and heavy rains. It's heading up the coast at a fast clip. The weatherman just reclassified the storm as a Category 1 hurricane."

"Oh my! When is it supposed to hit the area?"

"Tonight. You folks staying locally?"

"Yes. We're staying on an island—the one across from the campground."

The cashier stared at Aunt Claire for a moment. Then she said, "Surely you're not planning on returning to the island today... are you?"

Aunt Claire quickly nodded. She thanked the woman for the information and paid for the groceries. When they got back to the van, Aunt Claire said, "I think we'll skip the hotdog stand today. We'll go there the next time."

"...Um...Are we really going back to the island today?" Cheri asked.

"Yes. Our family has weathered storms on the island before."

"Yes, but were any of them *hurricanes*?"

"...I'm not sure."

Chapter 8

When they arrived at the campground, nobody said a word. The three of them stared at the whitecaps out in the bay. The bay was completely different from what it had been when they left the island that morning. And the water was a lot darker. There was a stiff onshore wind now which would be against them on the way back to the island.

Aunt Claire broke the silence. "Well…let's load the boat."

"Are you sure about this?" Cheri asked. "We could probably find a motel somewhere around here."

"We'll be fine," Aunt Claire said hesitantly.

Cheri and Victor hunkered in their life jackets as their aunt steered the boat. The three of them got splattered by salt spray. Waves crashed into the bow as they made their way across the bay. With the rough water and the wind against them, the return trip to the island took twice as long as the trip to the mainland that morning. All three of them breathed a sigh of relief when Aunt Claire finally edged the boat up to the island's dock.

Victor tied the boat lines to a piling. Aunt Claire dragged the anchor up the rock beach and placed it well above the high tide mark. Then, as a safety measure, she and Victor secured the boat to the dock with a third line. After that, Aunt Claire said, "Let's hightail it up to the cabin. *Now.*"

The sky grew darker and rain pelted them as they made their way up the hill with the ice, water, and groceries. Like the boat ride, it was slow going with the wind against them.

Once they were inside the cabin, everyone changed into dry clothes. Then Aunt Claire and Cheri unloaded the groceries and placed the ice in the cooler while Victor got a fire going in the wood stove. After that Aunt Claire prepared an early dinner on the tabletop camp stove.

The mother gulls did not land in the clearing that night. And the young gulls didn't show up either. The island suddenly seemed devoid of wildlife. The two seals that circled the island each evening were elsewhere. And the Great Blue Heron that stalked the tidal pool each evening was nowhere to be seen.

Cheri, Victor, and Aunt Claire stared out at the rain as they ate dinner. Then Aunt Claire reached across the table and turned on the transistor radio, thankful she had remembered to purchase batteries at the grocery store.

"The storm has been upgraded to a Category 1 hurricane," the weatherman announced. "It is expected to make landfall along the coast of Maine shortly after midnight. "Winds could reach 80-90 miles per hour and the high tide could be 4-5 feet above normal, which could result in flooding in some areas along the coast. Residents are advised to remove lawn furniture, grills, and other objects from yards and place them indoors. Boat owners should ensure that their craft is properly secured. Stay tuned for updates."

Aunt Claire furrowed her brow. Then she got up, pulled on her boots and donned her raincoat. "I'm going to check on the boat," she announced.

"Now?" Cheri asked.

"Yes."

"But you already took care of the boat. That boat is secure."

"You can never be too careful," Aunt Claire remarked. "I'll tell you a story about a boat that got away when I get back."

Aunt Claire returned fifteen minutes later. The wind blew the door shut behind her as she stepped inside the cabin. She was dripping wet.

Victor was stoking the fire in the wood stove. Cheri was reading her Nancy Drew mystery. They looked up at their aunt. "Is the boat okay?" Cheri inquired.

Aunt Claire nodded. "Yes, the boat is doing fine. There's nothing more we can do."

"How about that story?" Victor asked.

"You got it. Just let me change into some dry clothes first. Cheri, perhaps you could make us a pot of tea on the camp stove."

"Sure thing."

Ten minutes later the three of them were sitting on camp chairs around the wood stove. They sipped tea as rain pelted the cabin's roof. "Can you tell us the story now?" Victor asked.

Aunt Claire smiled. She ruffled Victor's hair and said, "You bet." Then she drifted back over the years to the summer she was twelve…

Chapter 9

The weekly trip to town had gone well. Claire and her younger sister went to the library to sign books out that day. After leaving the library they went to the dime store and bought penny candy. Their brother Curtis spent his time at the town pier fishing for mackerel. Meanwhile, their parents bought groceries.

The tide was dead low when the family got back to the island that day. They couldn't tie the boat to the dock. The dock was high and dry. They'd have to wait until the tide came in before they could tie the boat to the dock.

Their father tossed the anchor out onto the mud flats. Everyone hopped out of the boat and carried the groceries, ice, and water jugs across the mud flats, up the beach, and then up the hill to the cabin. On the way up to the cabin, their father pulled Curtis aside.

"Keep an eye on the boat this afternoon," he instructed. "When the tide rises, pull the anchor higher up on shore. Then, when the tide is all the way up, tie the boat to the dock."

Curtis nodded. "No problem, Dad. I know the routine."

"Thanks, son."

After the ice and groceries were unloaded, Claire and her sister went down to the tidal pool. Their parents worked around the cabin. Curtis headed down to the point to work on the raft he was constructing.

Since arriving on the island that summer, Curtis had scrounged for lumber and pulpwood—eight-foot logs that had washed up on the island's shoreline. After days of searching for pulpwood logs and lumber he finally had enough for a raft.

Curtis couldn't see the boat from his position on the point, so he walked over to the island's eastern shoreline and checked on the boat off and on during the course of his work. The tide was still way out each time he checked and there was no need to drag the anchor higher up on the shoreline yet. It would be hours until the tide was high enough to tie the boat to the dock. The dock was still high and dry, well above the water line.

Curtis got caught up in his work as the afternoon went on, the way one does when he or she is absorbed in a project. The first step was to place the logs side by side on flat ground. Then, he cut two ten-foot boards in half and laid each piece crosswise over the logs. The final step was to nail the boards to the logs.

Curtis eventually lost track of time as he constructed the raft. The next thing he knew, the sun was going down. He nailed the last nail in and headed up to the cabin for dinner.

After dinner, Curtis headed over to his cot. He lay down on his cot and began to read a comic book. It had been a long day, and he had worked hard. His eyelids grew heavy. He put the comic book on the floor underneath his cot and closed his eyes. Curtis enjoyed a deep sleep that night.

*****

The seagulls woke Curtis the following morning with their cries. He squinted at the early morning sunlight streaming in through the cabin's side window. And he suddenly remembered.

The boat!

Curtis got up and quickly pulled on his boots. Then he bolted out of the cabin and ran down the hill to the island's eastern shoreline…The boat was gone.

Oh no! Panic set in.

Curtis ran back to the cabin and woke his parents. "The boat is gone!" he cried.

His father rubbed the sleep from his eyes as he woke. Then he said, "*Gone?*"

Curtis stared at the floor. "Yes…I forgot to tie the boat to the dock yesterday."

"Oh dear!" said his mother.

"We're stranded?" Claire and her sister asked in unison.

"Not to worry," their father said. "I'm sure the boat is nearby. Let's go look for it."

Their father grabbed a pair of binoculars and they quickly made their way down to the island's eastern shoreline. He scanned the area with the binoculars…but there was no sign of the boat. "Let's walk around the island," he said. "Maybe we'll get lucky and find the boat washed up on the other side."

The family walked around the entire island. The father studied the water around the island with binoculars as they walked the shoreline. There was no sign of the boat. "Well," he said. "How's that raft coming along, Curtis?"

"I finished it," Curtis replied.

"That's a good thing. When the tide is all the way out later this morning we'll drag it down to the water. You might be able to pole the raft over to the mainland and borrow a boat. I'm too heavy…but you could give it a try, Curtis. You'll have to wear a life jacket of course."

"Uh…sure Dad."

Two hours later, when the tide was almost dead low, Curtis and his father dragged the raft down to the water's edge. Claire and her sister trailed behind them. They carried a pole they had found washed up on shore. The pole was their contribution to the rescue effort.

"Be careful now, son. Just turn around and come back if the wind picks up or if you get into trouble."

"Okay," Curtis replied as he shoved off into the crystal clear water.

Curtis poled the raft toward the mainland. The water was very shallow at first and he made good headway. But as he moved further away from the island the water became deeper. And deeper. Curtis guessed the water was eight feet deep—only the last two feet of the ten-foot pole were dry…Then he saw a big drop-off up ahead. He couldn't see the bottom beyond the drop off. It would be much too deep for the pole. He'd have no control over the raft once he entered the deeper water.

Curtis poled the raft back to the island. The family would need to come up with a new rescue plan. There was just a two-day supply of food and water remaining.

The family had a conference in the cabin after Curtis returned to shore. A number of rescue ideas were tossed around. Swimming to the mainland was one. Another was using a mirror to signal planes that might fly over. Someone recommended breaking the raft up and using the pulpwood logs to write S.O.S. to alert passing planes. There was also a suggestion to place a note in a bottle and throw it into the bay off the eastern shore. Claire thought that everyone should run up and down the beach and wave their arms and shout for help in the hope that a passing boat might notice.

In the end, they tried everything except swimming to the mainland. The water was just too cold that far north, and the distance to the mainland too great.

A day passed. Then another day passed. A few planes had flown over the island but they were too high up to see the pulpwood S.O.S. A half dozen fishing boats passed by, but they were too far out in the bay to see everyone jumping up and down and waving their arms on the island's shoreline.

By the third day there was no more food and just a half gallon of water left. That afternoon everyone suddenly perked up when they heard a diesel engine in the distance. The noise was off the island's western shoreline. Claire got the binoculars out and scanned the bay. "It's a lobster boat! It looks like it's towing a boat...our boat. And it's headed this way!"

Everyone jumped for joy. Then the family bolted down to the rock beach and everyone waved their arms in the air. The lobster boat pulled up to dock five minutes later. There was a lobsterman in the boat's pilot house. He was behind the wheel. There was a boy beside him. The kid looked to be around Claire's age. The two of them stepped out from the pilot house and hopped onto the deck. "Hello there," the lobsterman called out. "Are you folks okay?"

"We are now! Thanks for returning our boat. We can't thank you enough. We'll be forever grateful."

"Glad to be of help. We found the boat washed up on another island up the bay. Thought it might belong to you folks. How long have you been without it?"

"Three days."

"My word! You must be hungry. Here, let me get you some lobsters."

"Thanks. This day keeps getting better."

The family made two new friends that afternoon. The lobsterman's name was Mr. Cooke. His son's name was Caleb. The two of them joined the family for a lobster dinner.

Mr. Cooke had been born and raised in the area. He was very familiar with the island's history. As they ate, he told them how people from the mainland used to bring their sheep over to the island to graze. He talked of an old well on the southern section of the island. He mentioned how sailing ships had stopped at the island to replenish their water supply in the old days.

Claire glanced over at Caleb as his father talked. Caleb was looking at her. She smiled.

After dinner, Mr. Cooke pointed out a circle of rocks beyond the tidal pool. He told them that the rocks had been part of an old Native American fish weir. He also mentioned how the island had once been a smuggler's hideout during the days of prohibition when rum runners traveled up the coast to pick up cases of scotch whiskey and champagne from Canadian ports.

Finally, after everyone had finished their meal, Mr. Cooke said, "Well, we've got to be pushing off now. Need to get the rest of the lobsters to the pound before it closes."

The family thanked the man and his son once more. They were thankful for their new friends. Very thankful indeed!

Chapter 10

Aunt Claire took a long sip from her mug of tea. Then Victor asked, "Did you ever see the lobsterman and his son again?"

Aunt Claire nodded. "Yes indeed. We saw Mr. Cooke and Caleb each summer after that. Lobster dinner became an island tradition."

Just then, thunder boomed outside. Cheri jumped.

"A little thunder and lightning won't harm us," Aunt Claire informed them. "We've weathered storms worse than this. Who's up for a game of *Go Fish*?"

"*Go Fish*?" Cheri asked. "What kind of game is that?"

Aunt Claire smiled. "It's a card game. Your mother and I used to play it all the time."

"Count me in," said Victor.

"Okay," Cheri agreed. "Let's play Go Fish."

As they played Go Fish in front of the wood stove, driving rain pelted the cabin. The wind howled. During their final round of Go Fish, a heavy gust of wind slammed the cabin. The walls shook. The mugs on the table rattled; utensils in the silverware box vibrated. Then thunder boomed. All three of them jumped.

"Um…are you sure we're going to be all right?" Cheri asked her aunt.

"Y-yes... We'll be fine," Aunt Claire replied hesitantly. "It's been a long day. Perhaps we should turn in."

"Okay."

The storm intensified as the night wore on. Cheri and Victor were on the verge of sleep when thunder boomed again. Then the cabin shook even worse than before. Wind-driven rain blew in through the sides of the windows and the cabin's roof leaked in several places. The three of them got up and placed pots and pans under the drips. It was well past midnight when the three of them finally fell asleep.

*****

Cheri woke to the sound of rain. She opened her eyes and glanced across the room. Aunt Claire and Victor were sitting at the table listening to the transistor radio.

"Good morning," Aunt Claire said as Cheri climbed out of her sleeping bag.

"Morning."

"The weatherman says the brunt of the storm has passed, but the rain is going to come down all day. This is just the aftermath now, though. The eye of the storm apparently passed over early this morning. It will be a good day to catch up on our reading."

What else can we do?

"Aunt Claire made oatmeal," Victor announced. "It's real good."

Yuck.

With the exception of a few excursions to check on the boat and several trips to the outhouse, they spent the day cooped up in the cabin. Aunt Claire read her novel and did some sketching. Victor played marbles nonstop. Cheri wrote a letter to Kara. Then she finished reading her Nancy Drew mystery and started reading another one.

At first it had been fun staying inside relaxing by the warmth of the wood stove. But by the end of the day, all three of them had *cabin fever*—they couldn't wait for the weather to clear for them to venture outside again.

Chapter 11

They woke to the sound of seagulls the next morning. Sunlight streamed in through the cabin's side window and warmed Cheri's face.

Finally!

Aunt Claire was cooking pancakes on the tabletop stove. Victor was down at the beach getting a bucket of seawater for dishes. He returned just as Aunt Claire flipped the last pancake in the skillet.

"Not a cloud in the sky today," Aunt Claire chirped as she set three plates of pancakes on the table. What do you two have planned for today?"

"I'm going beachcombing," Victor replied.

"I'll join you," Cheri said.

"Well, it should be a good day for it," Aunt Claire informed them. "Be sure to bring some firewood back."

"You got it."

Cheri and Victor headed down the hill to the rock beach after breakfast. Beachcombing was always fun—but it was especially exciting after a storm. There was no telling what might have washed up on shore during the storm.

It just took a few minutes to reach the rocky beach. When they arrived at the beach they saw a wide band of seaweed by the water line. It stretched along the length of the beach up to the point. Mixed in with the seaweed were numerous sticks, branches and boards. Victor and Cheri pulled the wood out and tossed each piece above the high tide mark as they moved along the shoreline. There would be no shortage of firewood in the days ahead.

Now and then they came across other things that had washed up in the storm: sardine cans, bottles, corks, a lobster float, a boat seat, lures, pulpwood logs (they thought about Curtis when they came across pulpwood logs), a life preserver, a wooden fish basket, and a section of fishnet.

They headed north toward the point. As the cousins rounded the point, Victor spotted a large object that had washed up just down the shoreline beyond some boulders at the water's edge. It was buried under seaweed. "Look at that!" he shouted. Victor ran down the beach toward the object. Cheri found herself caught up in the excitement. She ran down the beach too.

Victor was pulling seaweed off the object when Cheri caught up with him. She was out of breath. "What is it?" she wheezed.

"I don't know," Victor said. "But we're about to find out."

Victor carefully peeled more seaweed away…and they saw wood. Smooth varnished wood. Victor and Cheri continued to remove seaweed. They soon uncovered a rowboat.

"Wow! Can you believe this?!" Victor said. "It's a beauty…And it's all ours."

Cheri smiled. "That's right. *Finders keepers*."

"We could take it down to the tidal pool at low tide," Victor said. "And we could go fishing in it. It will be good for hauling firewood too." The possibilities seemed endless.

"Let's go tell Aunt Claire."

"Race you up to the cabin!" Victor bolted up the beach. Cheri tore off after her cousin. They ran faster than they had ever run before.

Aunt Claire was sitting in a camp chair on the front deck sketching a seagull when they reached the cabin. "That's exciting," she remarked when they told her about their find. "But don't get your hopes up. Chances are that boat belongs to someone. And they'll likely be looking for it."

Victor and Cheri sighed. Then Victor said, "Well, it's ours for the time being, right?" The kid was always so upbeat.

Aunt Claire nodded. "Yes, I suppose it is…for now."

They spent the next few hours removing seaweed from the boat and washing it out with buckets of seawater. When they had it cleaned up, Victor said, "Now we just need oars. We can use a pole for now though."

"A pole?"

"Yes. Like Uncle Curtis used on his raft."

"Oh yeah."

They were about to head down the beach to search for a pole when they heard the faint hum of a diesel engine. Looking out into the bay they saw a boat. A lobster boat. It was heading toward the island.

The two of them waited on the dock as the boat drew closer. Victor was all smiles. Maybe he'd get to go on the lobster boat. The kid loved boats.

The lobster boat reached the island ten minutes later. There was a lobsterman in the boat's pilot house. The man was dressed in dark green work pants and a matching shirt. The same kind of clothing some of the local men in town wore. He turned the engine off and the boat drifted up the dock.

"Hello there!" the man boomed. "I see you found my rowboat. Much obliged."

The smile on Victor's face disappeared. Cheri sighed.

"Caleb!" Aunt Claire shouted. She had just stepped onto the beach. She had heard the lobster boat too.

The lobsterman grinned. "Hello, Claire. How are you?"

"I'm well, thanks. How are you?"

"Great!"

"I see you've met my niece and nephew, Cheri and Victor."

"Indeed," the man said. "And I'm very grateful to these two for finding my rowboat. Thanks to you two, I am back in business. I use that rowboat to get to my lobster boat each day. I had to call in a favor to get a ride out to it this morning. I would have really been in a jam without the rowboat."

"Would you care to join us for lunch?" Aunt Claire offered.

Caleb smiled. "Only if you let me provide the meal."

"I won't say no to that. You know, this reminds me of the day we met—only this time *we* found *your* boat."

Caleb nodded. "I was just thinking the same thing."

*****

They ate lobster outside on the front deck overlooking the bay. The sun was out in full force and there was just a slight breeze.

Caleb updated them on some local happenings and events. He talked about the local seafood market. He mentioned the prices local fishermen were receiving for lobster, fish, clams, mussels, and sea urchins.

"People eat sea urchins?" Cheri inquired.

Caleb nodded. "Not the whole sea urchin—just the roe inside."

Yuck!

"I heard some people eat snails," Victor said.

"Snails?" Cheri asked. "No way."

"He's right," Caleb confirmed. "Up here we call them periwinkles. There's a market for periwinkles too. Snails are a delicacy to some people."

Gross.

"That's right," Aunt Claire chimed in. "When I was a girl, people used to gather them by the pail."

Caleb nodded. "They still do."

After lunch, Caleb looked at Cheri and Victor. "How would you two like to go lobstering with me tomorrow?"

Victor beamed. "Sure!"

"Okay," Cheri agreed.

"I'll pack a picnic lunch for you folks," Aunt Claire offered.

"Very good. Look forward to it," Caleb smiled. "I've got to be shoving off now. I have more pots to pull this afternoon. I'll pick you two up at the dock at seven o'clock tomorrow morning."

"Thanks. See you then."

Caleb headed down to the shoreline and tied the rowboat to the back of his lobster boat. Victor and Cheri watched from the hill as the lobster boat pulled away from the dock. They were sad to see the rowboat towed away, but they looked forward to their upcoming excursion.

Chapter 12

Caleb pulled his lobster boat alongside the dock at seven o'clock the following morning. Aunt Claire, Cheri and Victor were on the dock. Victor was holding his spinning rod. Aunt Claire was holding a picnic basket. Cheri held two life jackets.

Caleb stepped out from the pilot house and held the boat against the dock so that Cheri and Victor could step onboard. "Morning folks!"

"Good morning, Caleb."

"You're a fisherman, eh Victor?"

Victor flashed a smile. "Yes."

"Well, tell you what. There's a cove that's not too far from the lobster grounds. I thought we could go there for lunch. There's good bottom fishing for flounder in the cove. And when the tide is right—which it will be today—there's usually a school of mackerel around. We'll see if we can't catch a few."

"That sounds great!" Victor exclaimed.

Aunt Claire handed the picnic basket to Caleb. "I packed a lunch."

Caleb smiled. "Thanks Claire. We'll be back around mid afternoon. Okay you two," he said to Cheri and Victor. "We have some pots to pull. How about putting those life jackets on and we'll head out."

Aunt Claire shouted "Good luck" as Caleb pulled the boat away from the dock. Cheri and Victor waved to her.

They headed north. Flocks of eider ducks and cormorants lifted off the water ahead of them as they made their way up the bay. A half dozen harbor seals watched them from a ledge as they passed by.

Caleb called Victor and Cheri into the pilot house after a little while. "Would you like to steer the boat?"

Victor's face lit up. "Yes!"

Caleb positioned Victor in front of the wheel. The next thing Victor knew...he was steering the boat.

Cheri took a turn at the wheel too. She was a little hesitant at first, but soon became extremely happy that she could steer the boat on her own.

A half hour after leaving the dock, Caleb pulled the boat alongside a yellow and red-colored lobster float. Victor and Cheri watched as he gaffed the float, pulled it onboard, and guided the rope through the pot hauler. The pot hauler's motor hummed as the lobster pot was pulled up from the depths below. The next thing they knew, Caleb was hauling a lobster pot over the rail. There were two lobsters in the pot! Both were alive and kicking.

Caleb reached into the pot and pulled one of the lobsters out. Its tail thrashed and its claws came to life as Caleb tossed it into the live well. "That one is about a two-pounder," he said.

"We're off to a good start. This next one might have to go back though."

Caleb pulled the second lobster from the pot and removed a gauge from his back pocket. He measured the lobster and said, "Yep. This fellow has to go back. He's not quite big enough." He tossed the lobster into the bay. Victor and Cheri watched as the small lobster descended to the bottom.

"The pot hauler saves a lot of time," Caleb informed them. "In the old days lobstermen had to pull the pots up by hand. Well, one down…forty to go."

Not all of the pots held lobster. Some were empty. Others contained different species—sea urchins, starfish, and sculpins. The sculpins were odd-looking fish with large heads and big fins. Victor thought the sculpins looked prehistoric. Cheri thought they looked gross.

Caleb brought them to a cove for lunch. It was a tranquil place. The cove was backdropped by rock cliffs that were home to a flock of cormorants. At the top of one cliff was a nest that was far bigger than the cormorant nests on the ledge below it.

"That's an eagle's nest," Caleb said. "And look. There's the eagle now." He pointed skyward.

A lone bald eagle was soaring toward the nest. It was a majestic dark-feathered bird with expansive wings and a vibrant white head. There was a small fish clenched in its talons. "Probably going to feed her young," Caleb guessed.

Caleb dropped the anchor. Then he said, "Who's up for some fishing?"

"I am!" Victor blurted.

"Okay. I like your enthusiasm, Victor."

Caleb rigged two fishing rods. He baited the hooks with clams. Then he handed them each a rod. "Just drop the bait over the side and let it sink to the bottom. When the sinker hits bottom, crank the reel a turn or two. And get ready."

They did as Caleb instructed. A few minutes later the tip of Cheri's rod pulsated. "Um, I think I got a nibble."

Caleb studied the rod tip. "You have a fish on, Cheri. Reel it in."

Just then, Victor said, "Got one!"

"Splendid!"

The water wasn't that deep, and it didn't take them long to reel the fish in. A few minutes later each of them hauled a flounder over the boat's rail.

"They'll make a fine meal," Caleb remarked.

Just then, a flock of seagulls appeared at the mouth of the cove. They were flying low, hovering over the water. The water below them churned. "Mackerel!"

"Grab your spinning rod," Caleb said to Victor. "That school of mackerel is coming our way!"

Victor grabbed his spinning rod and unhooked the mackerel ig from the rod's second guide. Then he flipped the bail on the spinning reel and cast the mackerel jig…It fell short of the school. Victor reeled in and cast again. This time the mackerel jig landed in the school of mackerel—and his rod pulsated as soon as he began to reel in. "Fish on!"

The school of mackerel swam toward the boat as Victor battled the fish. Cheri, Victor, and Caleb watched the colorful torpedo-shaped fish in awe as the school swam under the boat. The mackerel were strong swimmers. The entire school passed under the boat in less than ten seconds.

By the time Victor reeled the fish in, the school of mackerel and the gulls had moved on. "We were in the right place at the right time," Caleb declared. "Good catch, Victor."

"Thanks."

They ate lunch in the cove. Afterward they headed back down the bay to the island. Victor and Cheri took turns steering the boat as Caleb filleted the fish.

Aunt Claire was waiting on the dock when they neared the island. Cheri looked over at Victor as Caleb edged the lobster boat up to the dock. Victor was smiling. The kid had been smiling all day. Cheri was happy for her cousin. And she had to admit that it had been a good day. It was interesting to see all the wildlife out on the bay and learn about lobstering. The fishing had been fun too.

"It looks like you folks had a good day," Aunt Claire shouted as Caleb pulled the boat alongside the dock.

"That we did," Caleb said.

"We caught fish!" Victor yelled. He held up two bags of fillets.

"Looks like we're having fish for dinner," Aunt Claire said.

"And lobster," Caleb put in. He pulled three lobsters from the live well and placed them in a box. Then he set the box down on the dock.

"Thanks Caleb. That's mighty generous of you."

Caleb smiled. "It's the least I can do after all the help I received from these two today. They are fast learners. Well, I've got to get moving. I need to get to the lobster pound before it closes. Thanks for all the help today, Cheri and Victor. You're both fine first mates."

"Thanks for taking us out," Cheri said.

"Yeah. Thanks very much!" Victor boomed.

"The pleasure was mine. See you later," Caleb said as he pulled away from the dock.

The two of them talked nonstop on the way up to the cabin. They told their aunt all about their trip. They talked about lobstering and fishing. They told her about the picnic in the cove and about the bald eagle, seals, cormorants and other wildlife they had seen.

"You two had quite a day," Aunt Claire remarked. "I think you'll sleep well tonight."

At dinner that evening they watched the mother gulls feed their young in the clearing beside the cabin. Cheri wasn't sure, but she thought the three young gulls by the jagged rock might have grown slightly since she saw them last. They were smaller than the other young gulls. They had been born later than the others. The three young gulls by the jagged rock had become Cheri's favorites. She had missed them during the storm.

Aunt Claire was right. Cheri and Victor did sleep well that night. They went to their cots shortly after dinner and lay down. The next thing they knew, sunlight was streaming in through the window and Aunt Claire was saying, "Time to get up. We're going to town today."

Chapter 13

When they reached town that morning, Aunt Claire parked the van along the curb in front of the laundromat. "First things first," she said. "We *must* do laundry." All three of them were wearing the last of their clean clothes.

Each of them carried their laundry bag into the laundromat. Once their laundry was stuffed into washing machines, Aunt Claire said, "Let's get some breakfast."

The diner was next to the laundromat. There were half a dozen locals seated at booths when the three of them stepped inside. They were greeted by the sound of cash register bells, country music, and the clank of plates and silverware.

"This place hasn't changed since I was a girl," Aunt Claire remarked as they made their way to one of the booths along the far wall. When they were seated, Cheri studied the songs on the tabletop jukebox. They were ancient. She didn't recognize any of them.

A waitress came over a few minutes later. "Good morning, folks," she said, handing each of them a menu. "The specials are on the board over the coffee urn. Can I start you off with some beverages?"

Aunt Claire nodded. "Yes, coffee please."

"Orange juice," Cheri said.

"Grapefruit juice," Victor requested.

"Sure thing. Be right back."

There were two locals seated at the next booth. Older men. Both of them wore the same type of clothing as Caleb—dark green work pants with matching long sleeve shirts. Victor's seat was closest to them. They two men talked loudly. Victor couldn't help but overhear their conversation.

"That sure is something about that fella finding a gold doubloon," one of them said.

"Ayuh. Lucky find," the other man responded.

"Of course, that wasn't the first. Others have found some over the years too."

"Ayuh. Seems like one turns up every decade or so. Always after a storm."

"Ayuh."

Victor listened intently. *Someone found a gold doubloon?*

The two men finished their breakfast and got up a few minutes later. As they were about to leave, Victor said, "Um…excuse me, but did you say someone found a gold doubloon?"

"Ayuh," the taller of the two replied. "A fella found a gold doubloon—pirate's gold—just a few miles from here."

"There were *pirates* around here?" Victor asked.

"There were," the other man said. "A lot of people think that pirates only looted in southern waters, but there were plenty of pirates around here back in the day. There has even been speculation that Captain Kidd himself may have been among them."

"Who was Captain Kidd?"

"He was one of the most famous pirates of all," the man replied. "There are lots of legends about buried pirate treasure on the islands here about. When I was your age my friends and I often looked for buried treasure."

The man handed Victor a copy of the local paper. "Here you go," he said. "You can read about the gold doubloon. It's front page news."

"Thanks mister!"

"Ayuh. Don't mention it."

Victor placed the paper on the table. The bold headline on the front page was hard to miss:

Local Man Finds Gold Doubloon

Victor's heart thudded with excitement as he spread the paper out on the table and anxiously began to read…

The morning after the hurricane started out like any other morning for local lobsterman, Harvey McCallisteire. After an early breakfast, he grabbed his gear and headed down to the rocky beach below his house. He was making his way to the dock to board his lobster boat when something shiny caught his eye at the water's edge.

"I thought it was just a shell at first," McCallisteire said. "I almost walked right by it. But then it struck me that it seemed an odd color for a shell. So I stopped and picked it up."

What Harvey McCallisteire picked up was a gold doubloon. It's no secret that pirates once patrolled the waters off the coast of Maine...

The article went on about Harvey McCalliesteire's find. It touched on the value of gold doubloons. And the story carried over to the second page where there was a picture of Harvey McCallisteire holding up his gold doubloon.

The waitress returned with their beverages. "You folks ready to order?" she asked.

"Yes. I think I'll try the banana pancakes today," Aunt Claire said, glancing at the specials on the board.

"Me too," said Cheri.

"Same here," Victor stated.

The waitress smiled. "That was easy. Coming right up."

After the waitress left, Victor asked his aunt if she was aware that there had been pirates in the area. Aunt Claire nodded. "Yes. Your grandfather was fascinated by the local history around here. I remember him talking about how pirates sometimes stopped by the islands around here to replenish their water supply and gather eggs."

"Did the pirates go to our island?" Victor inquired.

Aunt Claire took a sip of her coffee. Then she said, "It is possible that they did."

"I'm going to look for buried treasure as soon as we get back to the island," Victor said.

"I'll join you," Cheri chimed in. She was already thinking about all the things she'd be able buy if they found treasure. The two of them suddenly couldn't wait to get back to the island.

The waitress soon returned with three plates of banana pancakes. "You folks vacationing?" she asked.

Aunt Claire nodded. "Yes."

"Are you staying at one of the cabins down on the point? I heard they renovated a bunch of them over the winter."

Aunt Claire shook her head. "No. We're staying on an island."

"Oh? Which one?"

"The one west of the campground with the small cabin."

The waitress's eyebrows lifted. "You're the ones that stayed out on that island during the hurricane?"

Cheri nodded. "That's us."

"Well, you three are the talk of the town!"

"Huh?"

"A lot of people in town are talking about the family that weathered the storm on an island out in the bay."

The other patrons glanced over at them. Then the waitress turned and faced the kitchen. She shouted, "Hey Clarence. Come out her for a minute. These folks are the ones that survived the hurricane out on that island."

A rotund man wearing a soiled white apron stepped out from the kitchen. He walked over to their booth. "So you're the folks who stayed out on that island during the hurricane?"

"That's us," Victor confirmed.

"Well, that's something! I think that's a first around here," the man said. "We've had hurricanes before—but nobody ever stayed out on an island during one that I know of. You folks are diehards. Would you mind if I took your picture for the bulletin board?" The man pointed to a bulletin board on the far wall. It was covered with pictures of locals, many of whom were holding fish or lobsters.

"What do you say?" Aunt Claire asked Cheri and Victor.

"Sure."

"Okay."

"You may take our picture," Aunt Claire informed the man.

"Great." The man pulled his cell phone from the clip on his belt and took a picture of them. "Thanks."

"Thank you."

"I'm glad we came here for breakfast," Victor said as the man headed back to the kitchen.

"Me too," Cheri agreed.

"That makes three of us."

"So…we're kind of like…celebrities?" Cheri asked.

Aunt Clair nodded. "It appears so."

"Cool."

After breakfast they went back to the laundromat and moved their clothes from washing machines to dryers. When their clothes were dry, they packed them in their laundry bags and loaded the bags in the van. "We're good for another week," Aunt Claire declared. "Let's meet at the grocery store in an hour."

Cheri walked up to the post office to mail the letter she wrote to Kara. Afterward she walked along the waterfront and stopped in a few stores. Victor headed down to the town pier with his spinning rod.

*****

Aunt Claire was waiting in line at the middle cash register when Cheri and Victor stepped into the grocery store an hour later. "Hey you two," she called out.

They walked over and helped unload groceries from the cart. The same cashier was working at the cash register as before.

"You survived!" she boomed, loud enough for everyone around them to hear.

"We did," Aunt Claire acknowledged.

"Hey Mac," the cashier said to the man working the register across from her. "These are the people I told you about. The ones that stayed out on that island during the hurricane."

Mac looked over at the three of them. He took his cap off and scratched his head. "You *really* stayed out there on an island in the bay during the storm?"

"That's right," Victor said.

"That's something. Yer cabin's still intact?"

Aunt Claire nodded. "It is."

The cashier said, "I heard there was a reporter looking to do a story about you folks. You'll probably be hearing from her."

Wow! Now we're really going to be celebrities, Cheri thought.

Aunt Claire waved her hand in the air. "Oh, it wasn't really that big a deal…once the wind died down a bit."

Aunt Claire paid for the groceries. They brought the groceries out to the van and loaded them in the back. Then they boarded the van. Aunt Claire inserted the key in the ignition and turned it…The van wouldn't start. "Oh dear."

Victor and Cheri did not go treasure hunting that day. Between arranging for the van to be towed to the local garage and having it repaired—the mechanic replaced the alternator, battery,

76

and fan belt—there was time for little else. Getting the van repaired had taken up most of the afternoon. The three of them got back to the island just before sundown.

After dinner that night Aunt Claire said, "There is a book about pirates on the book shelf. It's an old book, probably out of print. Your grandfather picked it up at barn sale years ago."

Cheri and Victor went over to the book shelf and looked over the titles. Most of the books were paperbacks and there were some hardcover books too. They didn't see any titles referring to pirates, but an old leather-covered book caught Cheri's attention. She removed it and opened the cover. The title page read: *Pirates along the Maine Coast.*

"This is it!"

Cheri brought the book over to the table. She and Victor sat side by side and opened the book together. The pages were very brittle. Some of them were loose. At the beginning of the book were a series of hand-drawn pictures: maps of the Maine coast, pirate ships and treasure chests.

After flipping through several pages of pictures, they began to read.

A few minutes later, Cheri said, "The author mentions that pirates used to hide out on some of the islands in this area."

They read on. Then Victor said, "It says here that legend has it that there is hidden treasure on some of the islands! I sure wish we had a treasure map."

Aunt Claire looked up from her novel. "Your grandfather thought treasure maps were mostly folklore," she said. "He believed that most pirates didn't use treasure maps. He did believe that pirates marked the location of their treasure though. He had a theory about how pirates marked buried treasure, in fact."

"What was grandpa's theory?"

"He thought that pirates used *markers* to mark the location of buried treasure."

"Markers?"

"Certain objects," Aunt Claire clarified.

"Like what?"

"Well, he believed that pirates might have marked the location of their treasure with something unusual. He thought pirates may have planted a tree or bush over buried treasure—a tree or bush that was not native to the area. He also suspected that pirates might have marked their treasure with a formation of rocks—rocks different from those in the surrounding area."

"I can't wait to go treasure hunting tomorrow," Victor said.

"Me too," Cheri yawned.

*****

Cheri was on the edge of sleep later that night when she heard an odd noise…A distant clanging. A bell. A ship's bell…An old fashioned ship's bell…Like the kind used on old sailing ships…And pirate ships.

Victor heard the bell too.

The two of them drifted off to sleep that night with visions of pirate ships and buried treasure.

Chapter 14

Cheri woke up earlier than usual the following morning—but not as early as Victor. Victor was already dressed for the day when Cheri climbed out of her sleeping bag. Aunt Claire was putting breakfast on the table.

"I can't wait to go treasure hunting," Victor said.

"Me too!"

Aunt Claire smiled. "Sounds like you two have an action-packed day ahead of you—but don't forget to bring some firewood up from the beach. And we need two buckets of seawater for the dishes."

"No problem."

After a quick breakfast, Cheri and her cousin walked the island's shoreline to gather firewood. Then they went down to the tidal pool and filled two buckets with seawater and hauled them up to the cabin. Fresh water was too precious to use for washing dishes.

When their chores were done, each of them grabbed a shovel from the tool bin. Then they headed off in search of buried treasure. The sun was out in full force, and the whole day stretched out before them.

They started out at the island's northern tip and worked their way back, searching the low flatland of the island's northernmost region first. They looked over the area thoroughly and searched for "markers" that pirates may have placed on the ground to mark buried treasure. But they didn't come across anything that looked to be a marker.

After that they made their way up the hill to the high ground at the center of the island. They searched the area around the cabin and walked through the fireweed, but came across no markers there either.

Then they worked their way south. The southern portion of the island was not easily accessible. The terrain was a thick tangle of raspberry bushes, scrub pines and thorny gooseberry bushes. Short of bushwhacking, the only way to access the interior of the southern region was to follow the narrow seagull trials that meandered through the growth. And that's what they did. It was very slow going.

They had been making their way down an overgrown seagull path for some time, trying to avoid the thorns on the gooseberry bushes when they came to a small grassy clearing. The clearing was like a small island itself.

Cheri and Victor stepped into the clearing. They were glad for a break from the thorns in the undergrowth. The clearing was like a small sanctuary. Along the far edge of the clearing was a bush—a unique bush with small white flowers. It was the only one of its kind on the island.

The two of them approached the bush. The grass at the base of the bush was very tall and overgrown. Cheri brushed the grass away and noticed a white rock at the base of the bush. It was about the size of a brick. "This is interesting," she said, pointing to the rock. "I haven't seen any rocks like this on the island."

"And there are no other bushes like this on the island," Victor said, gesturing to the bush. He brushed some more grass away from the base of the bush. "Look! There's another white rock. And another!"

There were three white rocks in all...The rocks were arranged in a triangle formation around the base of the bush. Cheri and Victor looked at one another. There was excitement in the air.

"I'll bet this bush and the rocks are markers!" Cheri said.

"I think you're right! Let's dig here."

We're going to be rich!

The two of them removed the three rocks from the base of the bush and began to dig. It took a while to break through the grass. The soil below the grass was rocky. It was slow digging.

Forty-five minutes later, they had dug down only two feet. Then Cheri's shovel struck something solid. Thunk!

Cheri and Victor looked at each other. Then they peered into the hole. All they saw at the bottom of the hole though was a rock. Victor removed the rock and they continued to dig. They removed more soil around the perimeter and widened the hole.

When the hole was wide enough, Victor hopped into it and worked the soil at the bottom with his shovel.

Thunk! His shovel struck something solid. "Did you hear that?"

Cheri nodded.

Victor leaned down to see what his shovel had struck. He felt an object with a smooth surface. A metal object!

"Is it pirate treasure?" Cheri asked.

"I don't know."

A surge of adrenalin shot through them as Victor pried the object loose and pulled it from the bottom of the hole…It was an old metal bucket.

Cheri shrugged. "Well, it's *something*. Let's keep digging."

Victor nodded. There was only room for one person in the hole. He continued to dig. He removed another foot of soil…Thunk!

"There's something else down here," Victor announced.

Cheri waited anxiously as Victor reached down into the hole and removed an old ladle from the bottom of the hole. The ladle had a long handle.

"It looks like a dipper."

"Yes. I think it is a dipper."

"Do you want me to dig for a while?" Cheri asked.

"Okay."

Victor climbed out of the hole. Then Cheri eased herself into the hole. She dug down another six inches. Thunk!

"There's something else down here!"

Cheri reached down and pried a large rock loose from the bottom of the hole. She pulled it out and handed it up to Victor. The next thing she knew…her feet were wet. There was water in the bottom of the hole. "Um…I hit water."

"Water?"

"That's right," Cheri said as she climbed out of the hole.

They peered down into the hole. The bottom was under water now. Cheri looked at the bucket. Then she looked at the dipper. "You know, I think this is an old well."

Victor nodded. "I think you're right."

"Let's go and tell Aunt Claire about it," Cheri said.

*****

"That's wonderful!" Aunt Claire remarked when she heard the news. "Imagine if we can get fresh water from that old well. We wouldn't have to lug all those jugs of water over with us each time we come over to the island. Wouldn't that be something? I'll bring a sample of the water home and have it tested to see if it's okay to drink."

"I guess we found a different kind of treasure," Victor put in.

"Indeed you did. Great job, you two!"

"Thanks, Aunt Claire."

"This calls for a celebration. I'm going to make raspberry cobbler! I picked some raspberries while you two were out treasure hunting."

*****

Cheri heard the ship's bell again that night just before she fell asleep. "Did you hear that?" she whispered to Victor.

"Yes."

The cousins imagined pirate ships materializing through the mist on the bay as they drifted off to sleep.

Chapter 15

Aunt Claire was up earlier than usual the following morning. Cheri and Victor woke to the aroma of waffles. "Good morning, you two," Aunt Claire said as they climbed out of their sleeping bags.

"Morning," Victor said, rubbing the sleep from his eyes.

"Why are you up so early today?" Cheri yawned.

Aunt Claire smiled. "I have something planned for us. We need to get an early start. If we leave soon, the tide will be in our favor."

"Where are we going?"

"To another island."

"*Another* island?"

Aunt Claire nodded. "That's right. Snowshoe Island. It's just up the bay. Snowshoe Island is about three miles from here."

"Does this have anything to do with pirates?" Victor asked.

"Actually," Aunt Claire replied, "it does. But we're going there for another reason too—blueberries. We used to pick blueberries there when I was your age. It's still too early to pick blueberries, but I want to see if they're as plentiful as before. We'll plan to go back later in the summer if they are."

"Let's go!" Victor boomed.

Aunt Claire flashed another smile. "Right after you eat your reakfast."

*****

There was little wind that morning. The sky was overcast, ut the surface of the bay was surprisingly smooth. They made ood time until the outboard motor conked out.

"Oh darn."

Everything was suddenly silent without the hum of the utboard motor. While Aunt Claire inspected the motor, Cheri eard the ship's bell again. "Did you hear that?" she asked her ousin.

Victor nodded. The clanging sound was emanating from the orth. They looked northward...but all they saw in the distance vas a red buoy. A channel marker. It was shaped like a salt shaker. t bobbed in the current...The bell at the top of the buoy clanged ach time the buoy bobbed. Mystery solved.

"Aah," Aunt Claire said. "The fuel line is loose. That's an asy fix." She re-secured the end of the fuel line to the fuel tank. he outboard motor chugged back to life on the first pull and they ontinued up the bay.

As they neared Snowshoe Island, Cheri and Victor uddenly understood the origin of the island's name. It was simple. he island was shaped like a snowshoe. The northern half of the island was wide with a rounded headland. The southern half of the island tapered down to a narrow peninsula.

Aunt Claire pulled the boat into the island's southeast harbor. A few minutes later she turned off the outboard motor and the boat drifted up to a rock beach. The three of them hopped out. Victor dragged the anchor up the beach and set it down above the high tide mark. Then Aunt Claire grabbed a backpack. She slung it over her shoulder and said, "Follow me."

Cheri and Victor followed their aunt across the island's barren southern section and then up to the high ground of the northern region. They searched for *markers* along the way but didn't come across anything that looked like it had been placed to mark buried treasure.

The northern region of the island was altogether different from the southern region. Here there was lush green grass and a thick stand of birch trees. Beyond the birch trees was a field of wild blueberries.

"Wow!" Cheri exclaimed. "I've never seen so many blueberries."

"This is nothing," Aunt Claire said. "I've seen blueberry fields that seem to go on forever. Blueberries are an important crop up here. Some people rake blueberries all day long in these parts during blueberry season."

"People *rake* blueberries?" Cheri asked.

Aunt Claire smiled. "Yes, but not like you think. People rake blueberries with *blueberry rakes*. Blueberry rakes are shaped like a handheld scoop. A wide scoop with tines in front. The hardware store sells them. I'll show you one the next time we're in town."

"Interesting."

"Are we going to pick blueberries now?" Victor asked.

Aunt Claire shook her head sideways. "No. They're not ripe yet. I have something else to show you two though. Follow me."

The cousins followed their aunt down to the island's northeastern coastline. Once there, Aunt Claire led them northward along a thin strip of beach that buffered the Atlantic Ocean from the rock cliffs along the island's northeastern coastline.

Five minutes later they rounded a bend. Just beyond the bend was an opening at the base of a cliff. The opening—a hole in the cliff— was about seven feet high and six feet wide.

Cheri and Victor hadn't noticed the opening when approaching the island in the boat that morning. There was a large boulder a few yards in front of it. The boulder screened the opening from view.

Aunt Claire walked up the beach toward the opening at the base of the cliff. Cheri and Victor were just behind her when she reached it. They watched as their aunt removed a flashlight from her backpack and turned it on. Then Aunt Claire stepped into the opening. Cheri and Victor tentatively followed her. It took a few moments for their eyes to adjust to the dim light.

At first, they assumed the opening was just a small area that nature had carved out of the cliff over the years. But when their aunt pointed the flashlight up ahead they saw that the opening was much deeper than it appeared at first glance…It was a cave. The cousins stayed close to their aunt as she walked into the cave. They were twenty feet into the cave when Aunt Claire directed the flashlight's beam on the left wall. "This is what I wanted to show you," she said. She pointed to an old rusted chain. It was hanging from a steel loop that had been fastened to the cave's wall.

"What was the chain for?" Victor asked.

"I don't actually know for sure," Aunt Claire replied. "Your aunt and I discovered it when we were about your age…We guessed it might date back to the pirate days. We thought that pirates may have shackled their captives to the chain. When we were kids there was a rumor in town that someone found an old pirate sword in a cave on one of the islands in the bay. We always assumed it was found in this cave."

"Wow!"

"Is there anything else in here?"

"Yes. I have something else to show you." Aunt Claire pointed the flashlight toward the back of the cave. Just before the far wall was a large flat rock. The three of them walked over to it.

Aunt Claire shined the flashlight on the rock's surface. Victor and Cheri observed chips from a different type of rock on top of it. Victor picked one of the chips up. The edges were jagged but the surface was surprisingly smooth. Then Aunt Claire shined the flashlight on the ground around the rock. There were similar rock chips on the ground.

Victor got down on his hands and knees and looked them over. A few feet away, a small triangular-shaped rock jutted out of the ground. Victor picked it up and studied it. It had rough edges and a smooth surface just like the other chips, but it was bigger than the other chips. Victor suddenly realized what it was. "An arrowhead!" he shouted.

"Indeed it is," Aunt Claire confirmed. "Nice find. We *think* this cave was used by pirates. But we *know* it was used by Native Americans. They made arrowheads on that flat rock."

"Wow!" Victor boomed. "Can I keep it?"

Aunt Claire smiled. "You bet. I'm sure your history teacher will be interested to hear about your find next fall."

Just then came the distant rumble of thunder. "Uh oh," Aunt Claire remarked. "I think it's time to go."

Victor clenched the arrowhead in his hand as they headed out of the cave. He held onto it for the rest of the day.

Chapter 16

Cheri was beachcombing along the island's western shoreline two days later when she heard an outboard motor in the distance. Glancing up the bay, she could just make out a white skiff. Cheri's eyes followed the skiff. It appeared to be heading toward the island.

Soon the skiff drew closer and Cheri could see a person in the boat. An older woman. The woman appeared to be her grandmother's age. She was dressed in yellow foul weather gear. Fastened to her head was a wide-brimmed straw hat. The woman was wearing aviator-style sunglasses.

A short while later the woman pulled the skiff alongside the dock and turned off the outboard motor. "Hello there!" she called out.

"Hi," Cheri said.

The woman secured the skiff to a piling and hopped out onto the dock. She was surprisingly agile for her age. Cheri noted the woman was wearing the same knee-high boots that Caleb and the local fishermen wore. She assumed the woman had stopped by the island to go clamming. She had heard that a lot of locals went clamming on the islands.

"And how are you today?" the woman asked.

"Fine. Did you come here to go clamming?"

The woman shook her head. "No. The tide's not right. Perhaps another time though."

"Are you here to see my aunt?"

The woman smiled. "Indeed I am."

"Aunt Claire is up at the cabin. I'll head up there with you."

"Much obliged, young lady."

"Do you know my aunt?" Cheri inquired.

The woman shook her head. "Can't say that I do. I'm with the *Coastal Times*. I'm here on assignment. I'm writing an article about the family that weathered the hurricane on this island."

"That's us!" Cheri informed the woman.

The woman grinned. "Well, I look forward to hearing all about your experience."

Chapter 17

There were half a dozen people in the laundromat the following week when they arrived to do their laundry. All of them stared at Cheri, Victor, and Aunt Claire as they stepped into the laundromat.

After stuffing their laundry into washing machines, the three of them headed next door to the diner for breakfast. There were a dozen locals there…and each one of them stared at the three of them as they walked over to a booth along the far wall. A few of the locals actually tipped their hats and gave them a nod as if they were old friends. Strange!

The same waitress was on duty as before. "It's you!" she boomed, when she saw the three of them. "You're back!"

Cheri, Victor and Aunt Claire looked at one another in bewilderment. They had only been at the diner once before.

"You're *really* the talk of the town now," the woman said.

"Huh?"

"Everyone is talking about the story."

"*Story*?"

The waitress nodded. "You're front page news. See for yourself." She picked up a copy of the *Coastal Times* from a nearby table and handed it to Aunt Claire.

The bold headline caught her attention:

Adventurous Family Braves Storm on Island

Aunt Claire spread the paper out on the table as the waitress headed off to get their beverages. The three of them anxiously began to read…

If you happened to be in town or along the waterfront the day before the hurricane hit, you're likely familiar with the many precautions and safety measures that were taken by area businesses and homeowners to prepare for the biggest storm of the decade. Windows were boarded up, hatches were battened down, and many residents along the coast evacuated their homes. A number of residents in the area weathered the storm in the community center or in the emergency shelter that had been set up in the high school auditorium. But not everyone evacuated to safer ground. In fact, one family weathered the hurricane on an island…

The article carried over to the second page. It mentioned how the cabin shook at the height of the storm, and it touched on the storm damage up and down the coast. At the end of the article there was a picture of Cheri, Victor and Aunt Claire standing in front of the cabin.

They had just finished reading the article when the waitress returned with their beverages. "The owner said breakfast is on the house for you three today."

"Wow! Thanks," Victor said.

"Don't mention it. It's not every day that celebrities walk through the door."

*****

They received attention everywhere they went in town that day, from the grocery store to the dime store to the hotdog stand. It seemed everyone in town had read the article or had at least heard about it. It was a day the three of them would forever remember.

Chapter 18

Fourth of July

Cheri, Victor and their aunt were sitting at the table eating breakfast. The sun warmed their faces. There was hardly a cloud in the sky and the bay was calm. The surface of the bay was glass-like, in fact. The weather was perfect. It was t-shirt weather. The days had been getting warmer since they arrived on the island back in June. And this was the warmest day yet.

Aunt Claire looked across the table at Cheri and Victor. "Does anybody know what day it is?"

Cheri and Victor looked at each other. One day had blended into the next during their time on the island. They were on *island time*. There was no schedule to abide by. There were no deadlines or pressing events. Their time was their own to do as they pleased. They no longer knew what day of the week it was.

"Thursday?" Cheri guessed.

"Actually, it's Friday," Aunt Claire remarked. "But that's not what I meant. Does anyone know the *date*?"

Cheri and Victor shrugged.

"Today is July 4th. Happy Fourth of July!"

"Wow. It's already July 4th?"

"It is. And I'm making a pie today to celebrate," Aunt Claire remarked. "A Fourth of July pie."

Cheri's eyebrows lifted. "But there's no oven. How are you going to make a pie?"

Aunt Claire smiled. "I'll show you. But first, we'll need a cup of raspberries. I already bought the blueberries at the grocery store."

"We'll get the raspberries after breakfast," Victor volunteered.

*****

That afternoon, while Victor was down at the tidal pool, Cheri helped her aunt make an *island pie*. Aunt Claire placed a rectangular tin and a mixing bowl on the table. Cheri crushed graham crackers and sprinkled them on the bottom of the tin. Next they made homemade whipped cream by mixing cream, sugar, and vanilla in the mixing bowl. Then they filled the tin with whipped cream. After that they added blueberries and raspberries, in an American Flag pattern.

"It looks so nice. It's a shame we have to eat it," Cheri declared.

"We *have* to eat it," Aunt Claire told her. "It won't last long without refrigeration."

*****

After dinner that evening—when the last of the pie was gone—Aunt Claire asked, "Who wants to go see fireworks?"

Cheri and Victor looked at each other. "Huh?"

"Let's go see the fireworks," Aunt Claire said.

"It's too late to go to town," Cheri pointed out. "It will be dark out soon. We wouldn't be able to find our way back to the island."

Aunt Claire smiled. "Who said anything about going to town? Follow me."

Cheri and Victor followed their aunt down the hill to the island's eastern shore. The lights from the cottages on the mainland twinkled across the bay. Aunt Claire led them to the dock. She had set up three folding camp chairs on the dock that afternoon.

Each of them took a seat. They looked out over the bay toward the mainland and waited.

Minutes ticked by, but all they saw were the lights from the cottages across the bay. Another five minutes passed without event. They sat there for forty-five minutes, talking idly.

"Well," Aunt Claire said. "Perhaps I was wrong about this. Maybe they moved the fireworks further inland this year. We can go back up to the cabin if you like—"

Suddenly, the skyline across the bay lit up in a myriad of colors. There was a spectacular burst of fireworks. Then came distant booms, followed by more fireworks.

Some of the fireworks were shaped like palm trees. Others were star-shaped, and some were circular. Some fireworks left trails of stars that eventually petered out. Others cascaded like waterfalls.

They had front row seats to the best fireworks display that Cheri and Victor had ever seen. As the three of them walked up to the cabin later on after the grand finale, Cheri reflected back on the previous Fourth of July. She and Kara had taken the train into Boston to see the fireworks over the Charles River. They had arrived late and the field was mobbed with people. She and Kara had to squeeze in among the other spectators to sit down. The view was constantly obstructed by people standing up in front of them. And when the fireworks were over, they had to contend with large crowds and a long wait at the subway station to catch an outbound train.

Tonight had been altogether different. It was as if they'd had their own private fireworks display. Cheri just wished Kara had been there to enjoy it too.

Chapter 19

When they went to town the following week, Cheri walked up to the post office. There was an envelope for her. From the return address she knew it was from Kara. Cheri anxiously opened the envelope and removed a letter.

Hey Best Friend,

Thanks for the letter! It was sooo good to hear from you. From your letter, you are having a much better summer than me! It sounds like one adventure after another for you and Victor. How I wish I were up there on the island with you, Victor, and your aunt! You have done more in one day than I have done all summer! And those raspberry cobblers your aunt makes sound delicious. Yum.

The camp is closed. It never opened. There was an issue with the health department or something. And get this; we're experiencing a heat wave and the town pool is closed. A pump broke and the water turned green. It has been one boring summer here.

Please write again and tell me more about your adventures on the island.

Your BF,

Kara

Cheri folded the letter and tucked it in her back pocket. Kara's letter put things in a different perspective.

Chapter 20

The young gulls were in transition. Their peach fuzz was giving way to feathers. By mid-July, all of the young gulls—including Cheri's favorite three—had light gray feathers.

One day seemed to blend into another during the month of July. The temperature increased with each passing day. But as hot as it was during the day, most nights were still cool enough to warrant a fire in the wood stove.

Aunt Claire usually painted during the morning when it was cool. She gave Cheri and Victor painting lessons when they weren't beachcombing, reading, gathering firewood, exploring the tidal pool, clamming, fishing, checking on the scarecrow or just lounging around. They picked blueberries at Snowshoe Island during the last week of July, and they explored the cave again. There was never a shortage of things to do.

As July gave way to August, the fireweed turned bright purple. From a distance, it appeared that the island was blanketed in purple.

They went to town in the first week of August. After their laundry was done, Cheri visited the shops along the waterfront while Victor fished from the town pier. Aunt Claire went to the post office. There was a letter for her.

When the three of them were eating lunch at a picnic table beside the hotdog stand that afternoon, Aunt Claire made an announcement. "I received good news today. Several of my paintings have been selected to be displayed in an art gallery in New York City. There's a big art show coming up there later next week."

"That's great!" Cheri said.

"Yeah, congratulations Aunt Claire!" Victor boomed.

"Thanks…but there's more news too."

"Oh?"

"Our vacation is going to be cut short. I need to be in New York for the art show. We only have one more week left on the island."

"Oh…"

*****

It was late afternoon when Aunt Claire pulled the boat up to the island's dock. Cheri and Victor hopped out and tied the boat lines to a dock piling while Aunt Claire turned the outboard motor off.

As they began to unload the groceries, water jugs and laundry bags from the boat, Cheri suddenly had the feeling that she had forgotten something. She soon realized what that *something* was—her laundry bag. She had left it in the van. "Um, I forgot my laundry bag."

Aunt Claire looked at her. "You *forgot* your laundry bag?"

Cheri nodded. "Uh-huh. It's in the van."

"Hmmm."

"Any chance we could go back and get it?"

Aunt Claire shook her head. "Sorry, kiddo. It's too late. The sun will be going down soon."

"Can we get it tomorrow?"

Aunt Claire hesitated. Then she said, "We only have enough gas left for one return trip to the mainland—our final trip next week."

"But I need my clothes," Cheri pleaded. "All of my shirts and pants are in my laundry bag. Everything except what I'm wearing."

Aunt Claire said, "There are plenty of *island dresses* in the trunk."

Cheri frowned. "I don't wear dresses. I haven't worn a dress since kindergarten."

"Tell you what," Aunt Claire said. "Try on one of the dresses tomorrow. Wear it for a day. Then, if you feel like you really can't get by without your regular clothes, we'll go to the mainland the next day to pick up your clothes and buy more gas for the outboard motor."

Cheri sighed. "Okay."

Chapter 21

Aunt Claire had splurged at the grocery store that day—she bought three steaks. It wasn't every day that she received such good news. She felt like celebrating.

They ate their steaks at the cabin's only table that night. As they began to eat, the mother gulls started landing in the clearing beside the cabin. They called in their young for their daily meal.

Young, grey-feathered gulls left their hiding places and scurried down the trails in the fireweed that bordered the clearing. Once they reached the clearing, the young gulls eagerly made their way over to their mother for their daily meal. The clearing was soon filled with young gulls.

This was Cheri's favorite time of day now. She and Victor watched as the young gulls devoured their meal—all but three young gulls that is. Three young gulls stood by the jagged rock— Cheri's favorite gulls. Their mother hadn't shown up yet. The threesome remained by the jagged rock as the other young gulls feasted. Their heads bobbed up and down as they searched for their mother. They looked hungry. And worried.

The sun began to edge lower over the horizon. Their mother still hadn't arrived with their daily meal. The three young gulls stayed in the clearing after the other young gulls had finished eating and retreated back to their hiding places in the fireweed to settle down for the night.

"Something must have happened to their mother," Cheri stated. "Those three must be very hungry."

"I'll bet," Victor agreed.

"We could feed them," Cheri suggested.

Aunt Claire nodded. "That's a fine idea. I'll get some dinner ready for them."

A few minutes later Cheri and Victor stepped into the clearing. The three young gulls scampered into the fireweed as they approached. Cheri placed a cup of blueberries on the ground by the jagged rock. Then she and Victor headed back to the cabin.

After they left, the three young gulls emerged from the fireweed and cautiously made their way over to the blueberries by the jagged rock and ate a late dinner. Cheri and Victor watched them through the cabin window.

The three young gulls ate all of the berries. Afterward, the three of them scanned the area once more for their mother. But she was nowhere to be found. Darkness edged in and the three young gulls retreated back into the fireweed to bed down for the evening.

"I hope their mother shows up tomorrow," Cheri sighed.

"Me too," Victor said.

Chapter 22

Sunlight streamed in through the cabin's side window as Cheri woke the following morning. She squinted as her eyes adjusted to the bright daylight. Then she hopped down from her cot.

Aunt Claire was outside painting. Victor was off searching for firewood. Cheri made her way over to the trunk and opened it up. She hadn't looked inside the trunk since the day she rummaged through it back in June in search of clothing for the scarecrow.

In the middle of the trunk, amid old flannel shirts and jeans, was a stack of five neatly-folded dresses. It appeared Aunt Claire had tidied things up in the trunk since Cheri had last opened the trunk.

Most of the dresses were knee-length. All of the dresses were well worn but intact, with the exception of a few small holes and tears. All of them were cotton summer dresses.

Cheri chided herself for forgetting her laundry bag. *I can't believe I'm going to wear a dress.*

She rummaged through the dresses. After some thought, she picked up a lavender sundress and held it in front of her. It looked like it would fit.

*****

Aunt Claire looked up from her easel when Cheri stepped out from the cabin. "That was your mother's favorite *island dress*," she remarked upon seeing the dress that Cheri had selected.

Cheri frowned. "Where's Victor?"

"He's down at the tidal pool. Why don't you join him?"

"Okay. See you later."

The sun was to her back as Cheri headed down the hill to the rock beach. She felt the warmth of the sun's rays on her neck, arms and legs. It felt good.

Victor was knee-deep in the tidal pool when Cheri arrived at the water's edge. Cheri slipped out of her sneakers and waded out to her cousin. She found the dress was actually the perfect length for the occasion—unlike Victor, she didn't have to bother with rolling up pant legs or pulling on bulky hip boots to keep her clothing dry. And Cheri had to admit…the dress was comfortable. The cotton felt good against her skin.

"Hey, Cheri."

"Hi, Vic. What are you up to?"

"Looking for minnows."

Just then they heard seagulls squawking overhead. A flock of seagulls was hovering in the wind currents over a large rock at the far end of the tidal pool. Clenched in their beaks were shellfish: mussels, whelks and clams. Cheri and Victor watched as the gulls dropped the shellfish onto the rock. After each drop, the gulls swooped down and landed on the rock to inspect their meal.

Sometimes, the shells didn't open up so easily and the gulls had to repeat the process…over and over again. Cheri wondered if one of the gulls might be the mother of her favorite three young gulls. But that evening, the mother of the three young gulls by the jagged rock in the clearing didn't appear again.

After dinner that night, Cheri and Victor left some steamed mussels and a handful of gooseberries beside the jagged rock. This time the three young gulls only retreated into the fireweed a little way as the two of them approached. And the trio came out and began to eat before Cheri and Victor made it back to the cabin.

Chapter 23

The temperature dropped later that night. And the wind picked up. Cheri and Victor huddled deep in their sleeping bags. The cabin was colder than usual when they woke the following morning and the wind was howling. There were whitecaps out in the bay.

Cheri hopped down from her cot and made her way over to the trunk. She opened the trunk and surveyed the dresses. After some thought, she selected a light blue ankle-length dress with long sleeves. "Good choice," Aunt Claire commented. "That was one of my favorites. It's perfect for this cool weather."

Cheri nodded.

As they ate breakfast, Aunt Claire looked out at the whitecaps in the bay. "We couldn't go to the mainland today if we wanted to," she announced. "Too much wind. It wouldn't be safe out in the bay."

Cheri sighed. "We don't have to go to the mainland…I can get by without my laundry bag."

Aunt Claire looked at her. "Are you sure?"

"Yes."

The weather gradually improved that morning. And the wind died down in the afternoon as the tide receded. By sundown the bay was calm.

The mother gulls landed in the clearing at the usual time that evening to feed their young, but once again, the mother of Cheri's favorite three young gulls didn't show up. Cheri was starting to worry about the three young gulls. She and Victor would be leaving the island soon. If their mother didn't show up, there would be nobody there to feed the trio. They were too young to forage for food on their own.

Cheri and Victor placed some leftover mackerel and a cup of raspberries by the jagged rock after dinner that night. This time the young gulls didn't retreat back into the fireweed when Cheri and Victor approached. They remained at the edge of the clearing. And surprisingly, they ambled over when Cheri and Victor set the food down by the jagged rock. Then the young gulls ate their meal right in front of Cheri and Victor.

"Enjoy your dinner," Victor said to them.

"And sleep well," Cheri added. She wanted to pet them, but Aunt Claire had warned against it. She mentioned something about how their mother would be alarmed by human scent, if she ever returned.

"Good night, you three," Cheri said as she and Victor headed back to the cabin.

"You've changed," Victor said.

"Huh?"

"You're different now."

"How so?"

"Well, for one thing; you talk to seagulls. You never did that before."

Cheri smiled. "I guess you're right." She tousled Victor's hair.

Aunt Claire stepped outside later that evening. Cheri was reading a Nancy Drew mystery and Victor was engrossed in a comic book when their aunt called to them and asked them to step outside. The two of them went outside and stepped onto the front deck. The sky was clear. A full moon illuminated the nightscape.

Aunt Claire was gazing up at the stars. The Milky Way was visible. It was directly above the cabin. Cheri had only seen the Milky Way in books before. Back home the street lights distorted the night sky. It was a truly amazing sight. Cheri stared up at the Milky Way in wonderment. She thought it was one of the most magnificent things she had ever seen.

Aunt Claire pointed out constellations: Sagittarius, Lyra, the Big Dipper and Ursa Minor. She showed Cheri and Victor how to find the North Star. And then she glanced up at the moon. "A full moon," she said. "You two are in luck."

"Huh?"

"Tomorrow's low tide will be much lower than usual. It will be the lowest tide of the month."

"Why is that good?" Cheri asked.

"There's a sand bar off the northern tip. We'll be able to wade out to it."

"What's so good about the sand bar?" Victor asked.

Aunt Claire smiled. "You'll find out tomorrow."

Chapter 24

Cheri selected a knee-length faded cranberry-colored cotton dress from the trunk the following morning. She was no longer self-conscious about wearing dresses. It wasn't a big deal now, especially where it was just the three of them on the island. After all, her friends would never know she wore a dress.

After breakfast, Cheri, Victor, and Aunt Claire headed to the island's northern tip. Aunt Claire still hadn't provided any clues about the sand bar. She just told Cheri and Victor to bring a bucket.

When they reached the rocky incline on the island's northern section, they were afforded a magnificent view. The tide was almost dead low. Off the northern point, a sand bar jutted far out into the bay. There was a shallow patch of water between the rockweed-covered shoreline and the sand bar. "Let's go," Aunt Claire prodded. "The sand bar won't be exposed for long once the tide turns."

Cheri and Victor followed their aunt into the crystal clear water. It was ankle-deep. Cheri and Victor looked down at the bottom in wonderment. They saw coral. Pink coral. It was all over the sea floor. "I thought coral could only be found in warm southern waters," Cheri remarked.

"Now you know otherwise," Aunt Claire replied.

They walked carefully, doing their best to avoid stepping on coral. Soon, the rocks and coral on the bottom gave way to sand. Cheri noted brown discs on the sand. They were about the size of a silver dollar. "What are those?" she asked.

"Sand dollars," Aunt Claire responded. "*Live* sand dollars. We'll leave them be. We're after the old ones."

"Old ones?"

"That's right," Aunt Claire said as she reached the sand bar. She bent down and picked up a grayish-white sand dollar. She handed it to Cheri as she stepped onto the sand bar. "Like this."

"Cool." Cheri looked over the sand bar. There were at least a dozen old sand dollars on the sand bar. And the sand bar was peppered with other shells too: clams, mussels, sea scallops, periwinkles and whelks.

The three of them started collecting sand dollars. After the sand bar had been combed over, they waded in the shallows along the edges of the bar and came across more sand dollars. For Cheri, it was a welcome distraction from her worries about the three young gulls. The trio had been on her mind constantly as of late.

The tide started to turn not long after they arrived on the sand bar. "Okay," Aunt Claire announced. "Time to hightail it back to shore."

They gathered the bucket of sand dollars and waded back to the island's shoreline.

*****

"So, what are we going to do with the sand dollars?" Victor inquired when they got back to the cabin. Cheri had been wondering the same thing.

"Lots of things," Aunt Claire answered. "You can glue magnets on the back of them and put them on your refrigerator. We used to paint them. Sometimes we made sand dollar ornaments for the Christmas tree. One time we made sand dollar wind chimes. There are all kinds of things you can make with sand dollars. We'll pack them up well so that you can bring them home."

"Cool."

*****

Cheri was more worried than usual at dinner that evening. The mother of her favorite three young gulls still hadn't shown up. The trio looked so lonely by the jagged rock in the clearing. Cheri and Victor brought them a handful of blueberries and leftover fish from dinner.

The three young gulls actually scampered over to them before they placed the food by the jagged rock. The young gulls knew Cheri and Victor as friends now. Cheri and Victor watched the young gulls devour their meal.

When the trio finished their meal, they didn't retreat into the fireweed like before. Instead, they looked up at Cheri and Victor.

"Do you think they are still hungry?" Victor asked.

Cheri shook her head. "I don't think so. They ate a *lot* of food."

Cheri and Victor started to make their way back to the cabin...The three young gulls followed them.

Cheri saw them in her peripheral vision and stopped. The trio stopped and looked up at her. Cheri's heart went out to them. "I'm sorry," she said. "You can't come back with us. You need to stay here."

"That's right," Victor agreed. "You need to stay here so that your mother can find you."

If she ever returns.

Chapter 25

Cheri opened the trunk the following morning. She selected a pale blue cotton dress with sunflowers. Then she got dressed and joined Victor and Aunt Claire for breakfast.

Aunt Claire had gone all out for their final breakfast on the island. On the table was a platter of scrambled eggs, bacon, home fries, and toast. Cheri didn't have much of an appetite though.

The three young gulls loomed at the forefront of her mind. They were in her thoughts during breakfast. And she thought of them as she and Victor made a final trip down to the tidal pool later that morning.

Cheri became increasingly worried about the young gulls as the day wore on. Unlike earlier in the summer, she didn't think about what she was missing out on back home. Nor did she lament about not being able to use her cell phone or computer. She didn't think about herself at all. Cheri thought only about the trio.

The three young gulls were constantly on her mind now. How would they get by when Victor, Aunt Claire and she left the island tomorrow? The young gulls were too young to fend for themselves. Even if they were able to find a clam or a mussel, they would not be able to eat it. They could not fly. They would not be able to drop shellfish onto rocks from overhead to open their shells. How could nature be so harsh?

As they sat down at the table for their final island supper that evening, the mother gulls began to land in the clearing. Cheri just picked at her food as she watched the mother gulls call in their young for their daily meal. Once again, the three young gulls appeared by the jagged rock. The other young gulls in their clearing were bobbing their heads up and down in anticipation of their daily meal. Cheri's favorite three gulls just stood there hunkered down. They looked so sad.

"You're not eating?" Victor asked.

Cheri shrugged. "I'm not that hungry." She was saving her dinner for the trio. It was the least she could do.

Reality was starting to set in. This time tomorrow, Cheri and Victor would not be there to feed the three young gulls. Cheri's eyes were watery. She was on the verge of tears. And this did not escape her aunt's attention.

"Why the sad face?" Aunt Claire asked her.

"Those three are too young to be on their own," Cheri exclaimed. She pointed to the three young gulls by the jagged rock. "Victor and I won't be here to feed them after tonight. How could their mother just abandon them?"

"Sometimes nature has a way of working things out," Aunt Claire stated.

"But they're too young to be on their own," Cheri blurted. "They can't find food on their own. They need us. They'll have nothing to eat when we're gone."

Aunt Claire smiled. "Oh, I don't think you need to worry about that," she said.

She pointed to the jagged rock in the clearing. A mother gull had just landed on top of it. Wound around her leg was a section of net from the fish weir she had been tangled in.

The mother gull cried out with her feeding call. And the three young gulls quickly gathered around her and anxiously bobbed their heads up and down. Their mother placed their meal—shrimp—on the ground by the jagged rock. Cheri breathed a sigh of relief.

"All right!" Victor shouted.

As the three young gulls ate their meal, their mother looked over at the cabin. She saw Cheri, Victor and Aunt Claire through the window. She cocked her head. It seemed as if she wanted to thank them.

"Those three will be as big as their mother this time next year," Aunt Claire remarked. "Thanks to you two."

Now that everything was okay, Cheri's thoughts turned to food. She was suddenly very hungry. She had hardly eaten anything all day. Cheri dug into her dinner as the three young gulls devoured their meal.

Their mother stayed with them longer than the other mothers stayed with their young that evening. The three young gulls were the last ones to leave the clearing as usual, but under completely different circumstances than the past several evenings.

They would sleep well tonight knowing their mother would be there for them the following day.

After the three young gulls retreated back into the fireweed to bed down for the night, Cheri looked across the table at her aunt. "Aunt Claire?"

"Yes?"

"Can we come back here again next summer?"

"Absolutely."

"Great!" Cheri smiled. Victor grinned too.

"Perhaps your mother can join us next summer," Aunt Claire said.

Cheri nodded. "Yes. I think she'd like that. Aunt Claire, I have a question for you."

"Yes?"

"Could I bring the *island dresses* home…to wash them for next summer?"

Aunt Claire smiled. "You bet."